Books by Ed Dunlop

The Terrestria Chronicles
The Sword, the Ring, and the Parchment
The Quest for Seven Castles
The Search for Everyman
The Crown of Kuros
The Dragon's Egg
The Golden Lamps
The Great War

Tales from Terrestria
The Quest for Thunder Mountain
The Golden Dagger
The Isle of Dragons

Jed Cartwright Adventure Series
The Midnight Escape
The Lost Gold Mine
The Comanche Raiders
The Lighthouse Mystery
The Desperate Slave
The Midnight Rustlers

The Young Refugees Series
Escape to Liechtenstein
The Search for the Silver Eagle
The Incredible Rescues

Sherlock Jones Detective Series
Sherlock Jones and the Assassination Plot
Sherlock Jones and the Willoughby Bank Robbery
Sherlock Jones and the Missing Diamond
Sherlock Jones and the Phantom Airplane
Sherlock Jones and the Hidden Coins
Sherlock Jones and the Odyssey Mystery

The 1,000-Mile Journey

The Dragon's Egg

THE TERRESTRIA CHRONICLES: BOOK FIVE

An allegory
by Ed Dunlop

cross & crown
PUBLISHING
RINGGOLD, GEORGIA

www.TalesOfCastles.com
Cover Art by Laura Lea Sencabaugh and Wayne Coley

The dragon's egg : an allegory / by Ed Dunlop.
Dunlop, Ed.
[Ringgold, Ga.] : Cross and Crown Publishing, c2006
215 p. ; 22 cm.
Terrestria chronicles Bk. 5
Dewey Call # 813.54 ISBN 0978552342

"When Princess Gilda and Prince Selwyn refuse the offer of a gift forbidden by King Emmanuel, Prince Josiah accepts, not realizing that his actions will impact the Castle of Faith." –Cover

Dunlop, Ed.
Middle ages juvenile fiction.
Christian life juvenile fiction.
Allegories.
Fantasy

Printed and bound in the United States of America

That my heart would learn

to hate evil

and to love my King

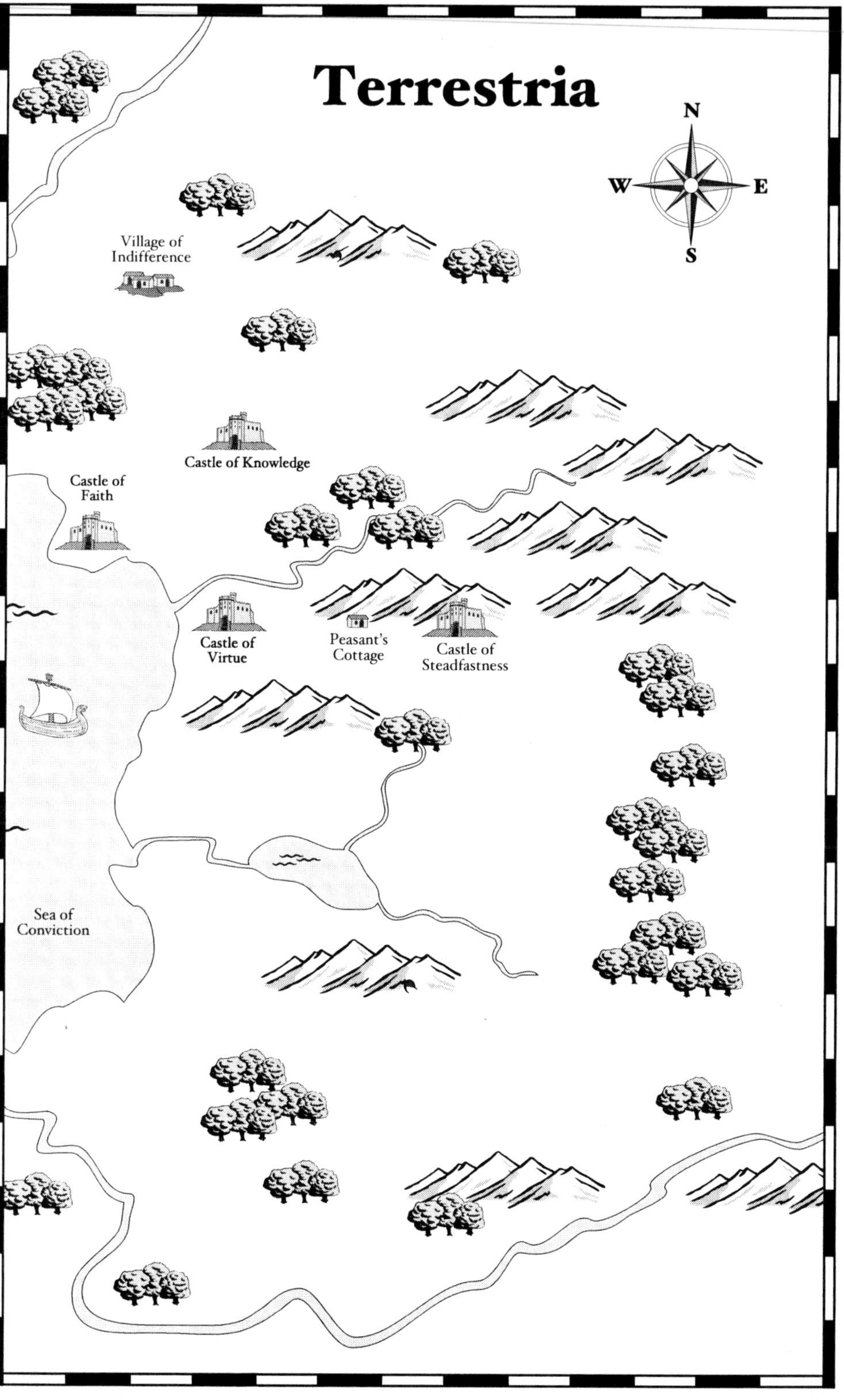
Terrestria
N
W
E
S
Village of Indifference
Castle of Knowledge
Castle of Faith
Castle of Virtue
Peasant's Cottage
Castle of Steadfastness
Sea of Conviction

The heart is deceitful

above all things,

and desperately wicked:

who can know it?

—Jeremiah 17:9

Chapter One

The scream cut across the stillness of the afternoon like the stroke of an axe. The sound was that of a woman's voice, shrill with the raw edge of desperation. The wail of distress echoed among the trees of the forest, and then, abruptly, silence followed.

Prince Josiah drew back on the reins and brought his magnificent white horse to a standstill. The young prince, clad in royal garments that identified him as a son of King Emmanuel, sat motionless, listening intently. Silence reigned. Even the birds sat motionless and quiet. It was as if time itself was holding its breath, listening, watching, waiting.

"The cry came from behind us." Prince Selwyn reined in beside Josiah and turned his horse. "Someone needs our help."

"Nay, it came from over there," Selwyn's sister, Princess Gilda, replied as she pointed toward the south. "Look!"

The two young princes turned and looked in the direction that she indicated. Josiah inhaled sharply. Two hundred paces away, dense clouds of dark smoke billowed through the trees.

"Help!" The cry came again, desperate and shrill. "Will someone please help us?"

"Come on!" Prince Josiah put his spurs to his horse and the

powerful animal leaped forward like a bolt from a crossbow. As the horse thundered down the forest trail, Josiah's two companions followed close behind him. The trail crossed a narrow, winding stream, which the horses leaped easily.

The three riders rode swiftly into a small clearing and reined to an abrupt halt. A small cottage was afire, with one end of its thatched roof nearly engulfed in flames. The fire roared and hissed like a wild beast intent on devouring the humble dwelling. Gilda sat motionless, wide-eyed and staring, but Selwyn and Josiah leaped from their saddles and dashed toward the cottage.

An elderly peasant woman ran forward to meet them, her eyes wide and pleading. "My lords, I beseech you, help us! My husband is inside the cottage and cannot get out! Without your help he will perish in the fire!"

"Stay here, good woman," Josiah told her. "We will bring him to safety."

Without giving a thought to the danger he was in, the young prince dashed forward, jerked on the latchstring, and flung open the door of the cottage. He leaped into the burning building to find himself engulfed in a dense cloud of smoke. His eyes stung and his lungs cried for air. Choking and coughing, he struggled to draw a breath as he peered about desperately. "Is anybody in here?" he called.

"Aye," a weak voice replied. "Help me!"

The voice came from Josiah's left. He turned, and, squinting against the stinging smoke, thought he saw a huddled form upon the dirt floor. Dropping to his knees and holding his breath, he crawled forward. An old man lay upon the floor, gasping for air. As the young prince reached him, the peasant grabbed the sleeve of Josiah's doublet in a desperate grip. "Help me, my lord," he begged.

"Sir, I'll have you out of here in an instant," Josiah promised.

At that moment, Selwyn appeared at his elbow. Seizing the elderly peasant by the arms, the two young princes hurriedly dragged the helpless man from the burning cottage. They laid him gently on the ground at a safe distance from the fire and then gratefully drew in huge lungfuls of fresh air.

"Josiah," Selwyn urged, "let's see if we can save the cottage."

Prince Josiah looked upward. Flames still leaped high into the air from one end of the burning roof, but, miraculously, most of the tinder-dry thatched roof was still intact. "If we hurry, we can save it," Selwyn declared.

"We can get water from the well," Gilda called, and Selwyn and Josiah turned to see a well nearby with two wooden buckets resting on its stone ledge. Rushing forward, Josiah dropped a bucket into the well and then cranked furiously on the windlass to bring it again to the top, brimming with water.

"I'll get the other bucket," Selwyn declared, as Josiah freed his full bucket from the hook.

Josiah dashed toward the burning cottage. Five yards from the front door he paused for an instant as he searched for a course of action. Gilda appeared beside him. "Here—take this and hand it up to me," Josiah said, handing her the bucket. He then climbed a sapling and stepped onto the roof. Gilda hesitated for half a second, wondering whether she should climb the small tree too, but then she saw a boulder at the corner of the house and scrambled onto it with the bucket, which she held out to Josiah.

Carrying the bucket of water, the young prince scrambled across the thatched roof toward the snarling flames. "Use this!" the peasant woman called, flinging a thick cloak up to him. Josiah immersed the cloak in the bucket, soaking up the contents.

Allowing the empty bucket to tumble down to Gilda, he sprang forward and beat furiously at the flames with the wet garment. A deluge of water cascaded over the fire as Selwyn hurled a bucketful from the ground below.

The three young people fought the fire valiantly, with Josiah beating at the flames from his position on the roof and Gilda and Selwyn hurling buckets of water from below. After several minutes of intense activity, the fire was extinguished.

"We did it!" Princess Gilda cried in delight. "We saved the cottage!"

Thoroughly exhausted, Josiah dropped to a seat on the peak of the thatched roof to catch his breath. His sides heaved as he studied the roof. Here and there, wispy fingers of steam and smoke curled upward from the straw, but to his amazement, he could see no damage to the roof. The straw had not been burned. He frowned as he thought it over. It just didn't make sense—the thatched roof had been ablaze for several minutes, and yet, the straw had not been consumed. Carrying the sodden cloak, he stepped to the edge of the roof and climbed back down the sapling.

"My lords and my lady, how can we ever express our gratitude?" The peasant couple danced about with delight. "You have saved our home!" the tall, thin man declared. He repeatedly threw his hands into the air and jumped about for joy. He seized Selwyn's hand, shaking it enthusiastically. "We are grateful, my lords and my lady. We will never forget what you have done for us."

Prince Josiah stared at him, amazed at the peasant's miraculous recovery. *Moments ago this man appeared to be completely overcome by the smoke from the fire,* he told himself, *but now he seems to be surprisingly vigorous. It is as if the fire has not affected him at all. How could he possibly recover so quickly?*

"We were happy to help," Prince Selwyn told the tall peasant. "As the children of His Majesty, King Emmanuel, it was simply our duty to help you in his name, that we might honor him. We are grateful that we could be of service to you, sir."

"Be that as it may, my lord, we are grateful," the man replied. "You have saved my life and you have saved our cottage. You three risked your lives for us, and we will never forget what you have done. Aye, you have indeed honored the name of King Emmanuel." The peasant's face was lined with the years of age, but his eyes glowed with the intensity and eagerness of a younger man.

The peasant woman hugged Gilda. "You three have saved my husband and my home," she said, wiping away tears of gratitude. "How can we ever thank you properly?" She hugged the princess again. "Thank you, my lady, thank you."

The man turned toward the cottage. "Please, my lords and my lady, do us the honor of entering our humble abode. We must express our gratitude to you with a tangible reward. Words alone are simply not enough."

"We want no reward, sir," Josiah told him. "We are thankful that we were able to save you from the fire, and we are very glad that your cottage did not burn to the ground. That alone is reward enough."

But the peasant couple was insistent. "Please, allow us this honor," they said in unison. "Please, come in." Gilda, Josiah, and Selwyn followed them inside the humble cottage.

Josiah looked about the little cottage. The tiny dwelling was empty of any furniture or embellishments other than a hand-wrought table, two hand-wrought chairs, and a large, brass-bound trunk upon the floor. There was no fireplace, no cooking utensils, none of the implements of daily life. Josiah frowned. Although the two tiny windows were closed, there was no smoke from the fire. The room had cleared completely.

"We have only one possession of any value, my lords and my lady," the peasant was saying, "but it has no equal in the entire kingdom. Allow us to show it to you." With these words, he stepped to the brass-bound trunk, opened it, and lifted out a smaller chest, also made of brass. Proudly, he carried it to the table and set it down carefully, as though it contained a rare and fragile treasure.

He looked expectantly at his royal visitors. Placing his hands upon the small brass chest, he paused for a moment, as if to ascertain that they grasped the significance of what they were about to see. "My lords and my lady," he said solemnly, "behold our most precious treasure!" As he slowly opened the lid, Josiah, Selwyn and Gilda leaned forward.

The small brass chest was filled with straw. From deep within the straw a strange light glowed and pulsated with intermittent hues of blue and gold. The tall peasant parted the straw with his fingertips, reached deep within the chest, and proudly lifted a glowing object. Gently, reverently, he placed it in the center of the table. "My lords and my lady," he said, speaking in a voice hushed with awe, "behold the rare treasure of which we spoke. It has no equal—no one in all the kingdom of Terrestria possesses a treasure such as this!"

Gilda, Selwyn, and Josiah stared. At last, Gilda spoke. "What—what is it?"

The unusual object was elliptical in shape, seven or eight inches long, and golden in color, with iridescent highlights of translucent blues and greens. As they watched, it seemed to change color, shimmering and pulsating with a soft glow which dispelled the gloom of the cottage.

"We want you to have it," the peasant said softly, almost reluctantly, as if it pained him to part with his most prized possession. "We are poor folks, my lords and my lady, and we have no other way of showing our gratitude."

"What is it?" Gilda asked again, in a quiet, subdued voice.

"It is the egg of a Cararian Greatwing," the man replied proudly. "The last of its kind. As I told you, there is none other like it in all of Terrestria."

"We want you to have it," the peasant woman told them, her eyes filling with tears. "It has been in my family for generations, but we want you to take it as a token of our gratitude."

Josiah felt himself strangely drawn to the enormous egg. He stepped closer to the table, studying the mysterious object from various angles. The shimmering surface seemed to throb with a compelling rhythm, glowing and pulsating with iridescent light and color. He watched, fascinated, slowly becoming aware of the fact that the tempo of the pulses was somehow strangely familiar. He gasped as he realized that the egg was somehow matching the rhythm of his own heart.

"What is a Carair—Carure—" Gilda struggled to pronounce the name.

"Cararian Greatwing," the peasant said helpfully.

"Aye, what kind of bird is a Cararian Greatwing?"

"A Caraian Greatwing," the man told her proudly, "is the rarest, the most magnificent of all creatures ever to inhabit Terrestria. Any man who has had the good fortune to behold a Cararian Greatwing will never forget it, though he should live to be a thousand years old."

He lifted the egg, cradling it lovingly in his long, slender hands. "As my wife has told you, the egg has been in our family for generations, and it is our most prized possession. Today, we give it to you—as a token of our gratitude for saving my life."

"Nay, my friend, we cannot accept your gift," Prince Selwyn said boldly, stepping away from the table as he spoke.

"My lord, we insist," the man replied. "You have saved my life, and my cottage as well. The egg is the only thing of value that we have to offer as a gift. Please, do not refuse our gratitude, my lord."

"We accept your gratitude," the young prince told him, "but we cannot accept the egg. King Emmanuel would not allow it."

Gilda stepped closer to the table and touched the egg. Soon she was caressing it with both hands. "It's so beautiful," she said softly. "Selwyn, why can we not receive this gift at the hands of these good people?"

Josiah longingly eyed the glowing egg. "If they're willing to give it to us as a gift, Selwyn," he said, without taking his eyes from it, "then I see no reason why we should not accept their generosity."

Selwyn moved closer to his friend. "Do you not know what a Cararian Greatwing is?" he whispered. "This is the egg of a dragon! Possession of a dragon's egg has been expressly forbidden by King Emmanuel."

Josiah stared at him. "A dragon's egg? Are you sure?"

Selwyn nodded. "The Cararian Greatwing has been known throughout history as the fiercest of dragons. Aye, Josiah, this is a dragon's egg."

Gilda moved closer to the boys. "What are you two whispering about?"

"King Emmanuel would not want us to accept the egg as a gift," her brother told her quietly. "This is a dragon's egg."

"A dragon's egg!" Gilda said the words aloud as she stepped quickly away from the table.

The peasant laughed. "It's not about to hatch, my lady. This egg is more than two hundred years old. If it has not hatched in all that time, it is simply not going to hatch. My lady, you have nothing to fear."

He looked back to Josiah and Selwyn. "Will you accept our humble gift, my lords? The egg is our only means of expressing our deep gratitude. Please, surely you cannot refuse that."

"We accept your gratitude, sir," Josiah told him, "but we cannot accept your gift. His Majesty, King Emmanuel, has expressly forbidden his subjects to possess a dragon's egg, and we must never disobey his laws."

"The King need never know," the man replied slyly. "My wife and I will never say a word to anyone."

The young prince shook his head emphatically. "Less than two years ago I was the slave of the dread blacksmith, Argamor. His cruelty was more than I could bear, but I found myself helpless to escape my chain of iniquity and the weight of guilt, though I tried many times. Just when I had given up hope, His Majesty broke my shackles, set me free, and adopted me into his royal family. I am eternally grateful to King Emmanuel. My heart is yielded fully to him. How can you ask me to disobey my King, seeing what he has done for me?"

The tall peasant nodded silently as if he understood.

"If you desire to show your gratitude, sir," Prince Selwyn told him, "there is one thing that you can do for us."

"Name it, my lord, and it shall be done."

"Tell us how to get back to the Castle of Faith. We were returning from a mission for His Majesty and it seems that we had lost our way when we heard your wife's cries for help. Right now, we have no idea where we are."

The peasant smiled. "Simply ride toward the setting sun, my lord. You are due east of the Castle of Faith. Less than an hour's ride will take you there."

"We thank you, sir," Selwyn told the man. "And now we must be on our way."

As Prince Selwyn and Princess Gilda stepped from the cottage and walked toward the horses, the tall peasant placed a hand on Josiah's shoulder, gently restraining him. "Should you ever desire to return to this cottage for any reason, my lord," he said slyly, "simply ride sixty furlongs due east from the Castle of Faith. As you approach these woods, you'll see a tall spire of red rock. The forest blocks it from your view right now, but from the west it is visible for many furlongs. When you reach the spire of red rock, ride due north for three furlongs and you'll find the cottage."

Prince Josiah shrugged. "Thank you, sir, but I know of no reason why I should desire to return."

The peasant smiled, and a strange light played in his eyes. "My lord, I shall see you again within a fortnight. Indeed, you shall soon return to this cottage."

Without a word, Josiah stepped through the door and hurried toward his horse, troubled by the peasant's strange message.

Chapter Two

"A dragon's egg!" Prince Josiah exclaimed as he and his two companions rode swiftly through the forest on their way to the Castle of Faith. "I never would have known that it was a dragon's egg, had you not told me."

Prince Selwyn guided his horse onto a trail that ambled westward. "I don't think that the peasant intended for us to realize that it was a dragon's egg," he replied. "He mentioned that it was the egg of a Cararian Greatwing, but it was almost as if he was hoping that we would not know what that was."

"Wasn't the egg beautiful?" Gilda called, spurring her horse to catch up to the others. "Never before have I seen anything like it."

"A dragon's egg," Josiah said again, as if he could not bring himself to believe it. "I want nothing to do with dragons. It was just days ago that I fought the dragon Authades." He shuddered with the memory of the fierce battle. "Had I not been able to conquer the dragon with the power of King Emmanuel's sword, the Crown of Kuros would still be in the possession of that foul beast and my heart would still not be yielded to my King."

He glanced at Selwyn. "When you told me it was a dragon's

egg, my heart began to pound, almost as if I was facing the dragon Authades again." He shuddered. "I had this feeling of... well, almost a feeling of danger, as if the egg could somehow harm us."

"I also felt that," Gilda told him, riding alongside the two boys. "And yet, at the same time, I felt strangely drawn to the egg. It was the most beautiful thing that I have ever seen and I found myself desiring to have it."

Josiah nodded. "That's exactly what I was experiencing," he confessed. "I felt a surge of fear, and yet, it was almost as if the egg was calling to me. I couldn't take my eyes from it. When I went close to it, I experienced sensations that I cannot describe. I felt... excitement, pleasure, fulfillment. And I almost felt as if the egg was the source of what I experienced. Does that even make sense?"

Selwyn looked from Josiah to Gilda. "I think we all felt the same emotions. But remember, Josiah, Gilda, this was a dragon's egg, and King Emmanuel has expressly forbidden the possession of a dragon's egg. We must be faithful to guard our hearts so that we never find ourselves desiring that which our King has disallowed."

"Were the peasant and his wife breaking royal law?" Wide-eyed, Gilda looked at her brother.

Selwyn nodded. "They were."

"Then do we report them?"

"I'm not sure."

Josiah shook his head. "I don't think that's our responsibility. This is between them and King Emmanuel. In the kingdom of Terrestria, each and every man is responsible for his own actions."

The riders came to a fork in the trail, and Selwyn reined to a stop. "What do you think, Josiah?" Months earlier, Josiah had saved Selwyn's life while on a quest for King Emmanuel, and the two had quickly become fast friends. Although two years younger than Selwyn and almost exactly the same age as Gilda, Josiah had soon established himself as a natural leader, and the other two often looked to him for direction.

"Take the path to the right," Josiah decided. "The other trail looks like it would take us more to the south."

"Sounds good to me," Selwyn agreed, guiding his mount to the right.

"Do you know when I started wanting the dragon's egg the most?" Gilda asked, riding between her brother and Josiah. "When I found out that it was the egg of a dragon, and that it was forbidden by His Majesty." She frowned. "I love King Emmanuel with all of my heart—why would I want something more when I learned that he had forbidden it?"

Josiah sighed. "I must confess that I experienced the same thing. The egg was beautiful, and I immediately found myself desiring it, but when Selwyn told us it was a dragon's egg, strictly forbidden by King Emmanuel, at once I wanted it all the more. My heart is surrendered to my King, and yet, like you, my heart desired that which His Majesty does not want me to have."

"That's human nature, I suppose," Selwyn answered slowly, thoughtfully. "Forbidden fruit is somehow more attractive than that which is lawful. When we learn that something is off limits to us, we want it all the more."

Josiah sighed again. "Let's forget the egg and talk about something else, shall we?"

Gilda pointed. "Look—the Castle of Faith. We're almost home."

Less than three furlongs away, a majestic castle of white stone glistened in the late afternoon sun. Situated high atop a rocky palisade that jutted out into a sapphire-blue sea, the Castle of Faith rose majestically above the surrounding countryside. With its high walls and many towers, the castle was an imposing edifice, visible from quite a distance. Four round towers rose high above the front wall, one at each corner and two in the middle, with similar towers toward the rear of the castle. King Emmanuel's royal purple standard with the cross and crown flew grandly from the top of each tower. A winding road climbed the steep castle approach to cross a sturdy drawbridge leading to the massive front gate at the northwest corner. Below the bridge, a water-filled moat abutted the wall. The Castle of Faith was protected on three sides by the sea and on the north side by the moat.

Moments later the three horses trotted up the steep lane toward the front gate. Chains rattled as the portcullis, a massive, ironclad grating, rose slowly to allow them entrance. Behind the portcullis, immense oaken gates parted in the middle and swung open to admit the three riders. A sentry on the battlements above the gatehouse waved in welcome.

As he dismounted, Josiah glanced at the sun. "It looks like we're just in time for dinner," he observed. "If you'll care for my horse, I'll report to Sir Faithful and then meet you in the great hall." Striding quickly through the main castle gate, the young prince turned and hurried up the stairs toward Sir Faithful's solar, taking the steps two at a time.

He stepped into Sir Faithful's solar to find the castle steward busy at his desk. The old man looked up as he approached. "Josiah, my prince," he greeted the youth with a pleasant smile, "how went your mission for His Majesty?"

"It went well, sire," Josiah replied. As he gave his report, the image of the dragon's egg seemed to dance in the air above Sir Faithful. The young prince shook his head and the image vanished. Perhaps it would be best if the old steward knew nothing of the egg's existence. Josiah decided not to mention the incident.

The moon hung low in the heavens, a huge silver crescent against a backdrop of black velvet. A myriad of stars glittered like a handful of rare diamonds scattered across the same black velvet. High on the west wall of the Castle of Faith, Prince Josiah restlessly paced the sentry walk. He heaved a tremendous sigh and leaned far over the castle wall, gazing at the moon's reflection in the waters of the Sea of Conviction far below. Hearing the sound of approaching footsteps, he turned.

A sentry approached. "Can't sleep, my lord?"

Josiah shook his head. "Not yet, sire. I thought the night air might clear my head, settle my thoughts."

The sentry nodded in agreement. "It's a beautiful night, my lord. Rest well." He moved on and disappeared into the darkness of the night.

Josiah approached the southwest tower and climbed the spiraling stairs to the top. Leaning out into the darkness of the night, he watched the surging breakers far below as they crashed against the castle foundations and then dissolved in a frothing mass of white foam.

"Why can I not simply forget the egg?" he asked aloud. "Why must it haunt me so? I have not been able to put the egg out of my mind since the moment we left the peasant's cottage."

A petition! I must send a petition to King Emmanuel. Reaching within his doublet, the young prince withdrew a thick book. As he opened its pages, they began to glow with a soft white light, growing steadily brighter until the tower was ablaze with light. He read an entire page, at once encouraged and strengthened by the words of his King. Withdrawing a small parchment from inside the front cover, he wrote a brief message to King Emmanuel:

"My Lord, King Emmanuel,
Tonight I am facing a compelling temptation that I do not fully understand and over which I seem to find no power. I humbly ask for your almighty help, my Lord, that I may continue to guard my heart and honor your worthy name.
Your son,
Prince Josiah"

Rolling the parchment into a tight scroll, Josiah raised his hand and released it. The petition shot from his hand and instantly disappeared over the horizon in a thin streak of light. Josiah knew that his petition had already found its way to the throne room in the Golden City of the Redeemed and was now in His Majesty's hands.

Closing the book, he swung it briskly in a tight arc and felt a surge of assurance as it became a glittering, two-edged sword. The powerful weapon, prepared for him by King Emmanuel, had enabled him to attain the victory in numerous confrontations with the enemy. Holding the invincible sword close to his side, he paused as it transformed itself into the book, and then replaced it within his doublet.

Having sent his petition, Prince Josiah recrossed the sentry walk, descended the stairs, and entered his own solar. But as he dressed for bed, tantalizing thoughts of the egg danced in his head, refusing to go away or be shut out. He sighed as he drew back his coverlet and slid into bed. *As soon as I have the opportunity, I'll go back and just look at it once more,* he told himself. *Surely just a look can't cause any harm. And then I can forget about the dragon's egg once and for all.* His mind made up,

Josiah quickly dropped off to sleep.

Three days later, Sir Faithful sent for Josiah just after breakfast. "Josiah, my prince, I want you to undertake a special quest for me, or rather, for King Emmanuel," the old steward told him as he entered Sir Faithful's solar. "This assignment is of a very sensitive nature, but I believe that you are just the man for it. Your heart is fully yielded to His Majesty, and therefore I can entrust this important task to you."

Josiah approached the desk. "Aye, what can I do for you, sire?"

"You must undertake this assignment alone," Sir Faithful told him gravely, "and it must not be discussed with anyone, not even Prince Selwyn. You will not have the benefit of his companionship, nor the strength of his sword should you encounter any of Argamor's men, but I know that you will succeed. Are you ready for such a mission?"

"Aye, sire, that I am. May I always be ready to undertake a quest for my King, Emmanuel."

The steward looked at him closely. "Your heart is fully yielded to His Majesty's will, my prince?"

"Aye, sire, as well as one can know one's own heart, I am yielded."

"Very well." Sir Faithful reached under his desk and withdrew a small parchment, handing it to Josiah. "I want you to take this to the Castle of Steadfastness. Give it to Sir Whole-Heart, the castle steward."

Josiah felt a surge of disappointment. The "special quest" was nothing more than the delivery of a parchment, which any messenger in the castle could accomplish. He had expected more of a challenge than this.

Sir Faithful seemed to read his mind. "The parchment is incidental to this mission, Josiah, for I could send almost anyone to make the delivery to the castle. The delivery will simply put you in a position to accomplish your real mission."

The young prince tightened his grip on the parchment, unconsciously taking a step closer as he did.

"I want you to find and talk with a marquis by the name of Sir Dither. This nobleman is very powerful and influential, and resides at the Castle of Steadfastness. For a number of years Sir Dither has been a faithful servant to His Majesty, loyal and committed in every way. He has accomplished much for the kingdom, all for the honor and glory of his King. Of late, though, we have had reason to question Sir Dither's loyalty to Emmanuel. At times, it would almost seem as if the marquis would rather be in Argamor's service."

"Surely not," Josiah rejoined. "Anyone who has served Argamor and then experienced the lovingkindness of King Emmanuel would a thousand times rather be in the service of Emmanuel! I know that I would."

"Sometimes the heart wanders, and love grows cold," the old steward said slowly, stroking his beard as he did. "When a child of Emmanuel loses the wonder of his or her adoption, he or she is capable of just about anything. Perhaps that is where we now find Sir Dither."

"What am I to do, sire?"

"The castle residents eat the midday meal promptly at noon," Sir Faithful replied. "I plan for you to arrive at the castle with the delivery of the parchment for Sir Whole-Heart some thirty or forty minutes before the noon meal. Sir Whole-Heart will invite you to stay for the meal. You must find a way to sit at Sir Dither's table and engage him in conversation during the meal. I want you to determine just where the marquis' loyalties lie—with King Emmanuel, or with Argamor."

Josiah felt a twinge of apprehension. "How am I to do that, sire?"

"Simply engage him in conversation. Talk over the affairs of the kingdom with him. You will soon see where his loyalties lie."

"But how?"

"Your heart is surrendered to His Majesty, and if the marquis is of a kindred spirit, you will soon know it. If his heart has been drawn away, you will quickly detect that also."

"But sire, I am so young."

"And that is precisely why I am sending you," Sir Faithful replied, with a twinkle in his clear blue eyes. "You are young—very young—and for that very reason I believe that Sir Dither will be quite candid and honest with you. Were I to send an older man, Sir Dither would be careful to guard his tongue. If he is indeed disloyal to Emmanuel, he would carefully conceal that from someone who is older. With you, I believe that he will be quite open and honest."

"How will I recognize this nobleman?"

"Sir Dither is short and broad-shouldered, with reddish-brown hair and a well-kept beard. His coat of arms is a martlet and a sword set against an azure field. You'll recognize him easily."

"A martlet, sire?"

"A martlet is a small bird, a swallow."

Josiah followed the castle steward as he stepped outside and glanced at the sun. "The Castle of Steadfastness is nearly two hours due east of here. If you leave one hour from now, you'll arrive approximately half an hour before the noon meal. I'll see you this evening at dinner; you can give me a full report then."

He put an affectionate hand on the young prince's shoulder. "Ride carefully, my prince. On this journey you will face grave danger, and you must be ready."

Chapter Three

Prince Josiah rode over the crest of a hill and reined to a stop. Before him lay a broad, emerald-green valley, alive with colorful wildflowers and tall stands of oaks and boxwoods. On the banks of a swift-flowing river stood an enormous castle of gray stone, the Castle of Steadfastness.

Josiah rode forward. When he reached the castle drawbridge, he stood in the stirrups and raised his visor. "Halloo the Castle of Steadfastness! I am Prince Josiah of the Castle of Faith, with a message for Sir Whole-Heart."

"Advance, Prince Josiah, and welcome to the Castle of Steadfastness," a sentry called from the gatehouse over the battlements. "We shall inform Sir Whole-Heart of your arrival." Josiah rode through the gate and dismounted, pulling the parchment from his saddlebags. A servant led his horse to the stables.

A tall, robust knight dressed in scarlet and white strode forward. "Sir Whole-Heart, at your service," he boomed in a voice that echoed in the gatehouse. "Welcome, Prince Josiah."

Josiah handed him the parchment. "Sire, a message from Sir Faithful."

The knight accepted the parchment. "Thank you, my lord. And how is my old friend, Sir Faithful? Is he in good health?"

"Sir Faithful is in excellent health, sire. He sends his greetings and regrets that he cannot come in person."

"Aye, it would be good to see him." He unrolled the parchment and glanced at it, and then turned back to Josiah. "The noon meal is served in half an hour. Will you stay and dine with us?"

Josiah nodded. "Aye, sire, that I will. I was hoping you would ask."

The tall knight laughed. "It will be our pleasure to have you. Meet us in the great hall at noon. I'm sorry that I don't have the time to entertain you, but I'm in the midst of a very important project. Please make yourself at home—feel free to tour the castle or just rest from your journey. Now, if you'll excuse me, I'll see you in the great hall in half an hour."

Josiah made his way across the bailey and took a seat on a stone bench in the shade of a towering ash. Less than three paces to his right was the castle well. *How will Sir Dither respond when I try to question him?* he asked himself. *What if he doesn't feel like talking? I still think that Sir Faithful has sent the wrong person on this assignment.*

"Come back!" a voice called from the other end of the castle bailey. "Come back, you wretched bird!"

At that instant, Josiah gasped as a large bird of prey dropped from the sky, and, with the spread of silver-gray wings, landed on the ledge of the well beside him. The bird, easily a foot-and-a-half tall, sat warily on the stones, looking as if it might take flight again at any moment. Twice it spread its great wings as if to take to the air, and then relaxed and folded them again. Josiah noted that the bird's beak was covered with a small leather hood and that leather straps were fastened to its legs.

This was no wild bird; it belonged to someone.

"My lord, can you catch her?" The urgent plea, uttered in a low voice, came from a nobleman who crouched some thirty paces away. "She's watching me. If I come any closer, I'm afraid she'll take to the air again, but if you can sneak up on her..."

"What should I do?" Josiah asked in a quiet voice. "She looks fierce."

"Move slowly," the stranger instructed. "If you can get close enough to grab the jesses fastened to her legs, we'll have her."

Josiah hesitated. "Will she bite?"

"She's wearing a beak hood, my lord, so it's impossible for her to bite. Please, my lord, if you can catch her... she's quite a valuable falcon..."

The young prince slid quietly from the bench and crept toward the well. Holding his breath, he extended one hand, reaching for the leather jesses. At that moment the falcon turned its head and looked straight at him. Josiah stood motionless. He waited for a moment, but the falcon continued to stare at him. He held his breath, afraid that the least movement would cause the big bird to take flight.

The falcon lowered her head and spread her wings. "Now, my lord!" the man called. Josiah leaped forward and seized the jesses. The bird was his. The falcon rose in the air, tugging against the jesses, and then almost immediately settled back down on the well. To Josiah's surprise, the falcon relaxed and folded her wings rather than fighting as he had anticipated.

"I am grateful, my lord," the falcon's owner said as he approached. "She's a peregrine falcon, quite valuable, but I've just had her a short while and she doesn't know me yet. I thought she was ready for her first free flight, but—well, when she wouldn't come to the lure, I just knew I'd seen the last of her."

"I'm glad that she didn't get away, sire," Josiah answered. He grinned. "This is the first time that I have ever caught a falcon."

The man laughed. "You did a good job of it, my lord." He extended a hand protected by a thick leather glove and took the jesses from Josiah's hand. As he did, the falcon readily hopped upon the glove.

Josiah stared. The man was short and stocky, with brown hair and a well-trimmed beard. The coat of arms upon his jerkin was that of a small bird and a sword against a field of blue. "Are you—are you Sir Dither?"

The nobleman was surprised. "Aye, that is my name. Do I know you, my lord?"

"We have never met, but I have heard of you," Josiah replied. "I'm Prince Josiah, of the Castle of Faith."

"It's a pleasure to make your acquaintance, Prince Josiah. And once again, I am grateful for your help in catching my wayward falcon."

"She's a magnificent bird, Sir Dither."

The marquis smiled. "I need to return her to her cage. Would you care to accompany me to my solar?"

"Certainly, sire," the young prince replied. "I would be honored."

As Sir Dither turned away, Josiah looked up to see a snowy white dove perched in the branches of the ash tree. "Guide my words, I ask."

"I have been, and will continue to do so," the dove replied in a quiet, gentle voice.

Josiah followed the stocky nobleman across the bailey, up two flights of stairs, and into a room in the northeast tower of the castle. Sir Dither's solar was modestly furnished with a featherbed and nightstand. Fragrant reeds lay upon the polished wood floor, and a huge tapestry depicting a knight fighting a dragon adorned the wall opposite the door. A tall, narrow cage stood beside the single window.

"I keep my other falcons over the stables," Sir Dither explained, as he opened the door of the cage. "But since this one is new, I'm keeping her close until she gets to know me." He put the falcon inside the cage and carefully secured the door.

A woman's voice filled the room, and Josiah turned in surprise. A small glass sphere on the nightstand was ablaze with color and movement. Josiah's eyes widened. A spellavision! The images of an attractive woman and a tall, muscular man filled the sphere. As Josiah watched, the woman sidled up to the man and lightly touched his arm. Her smile was coy, her movements seductive, and the young prince suddenly realized that the woman was attempting to talk the man into committing an act of immorality with her. He turned away in disgust.

"This year's coach is bigger and better than ever before!" a man's voice abruptly announced, and Josiah turned back to see the image of a sleek vehicle speeding across the spellavision. "You deserve this coach. You've worked for it. And now is the time to reward yourself with the vehicle you've always wanted. Your local merchant can help you obtain this coach at a low price. See your merchant today."

Sir Dither laughed as he passed his hand over the spellavision. The images within the sphere vanished immediately. "The spellavision was given to me," he said. "I must say that it amuses me."

Josiah nodded, but said nothing. *I think I know who was behind the gift,* he thought grimly. *It was given to you to draw your heart away from King Emmanuel. The spellavision is part of Argamor's plan to wrest the kingdom from King Emmanuel.*

"So what brings you to the Castle of Steadfastness?" Sir Dither asked. "We're some distance from the Castle of Faith."

"I'm on an errand for King Emmanuel," Josiah replied, with enthusiasm. "Sir Faithful sent me with a parchment for Sir Whole-Heart."

The marquis said nothing, but his face took on an unusual expression.

Josiah noticed. "What are you thinking, sire?"

Sir Dither shook his head. "Oh, nothing of any consequence, my lord. It doesn't matter."

"Oh, but it does matter, sire. When I stated that I was on an errand for His Majesty, your face took on a really strange expression. Your reaction tells me that something is wrong. What were you thinking, sire?"

Sir Dither rubbed his beard. "All right. You asked, so I'll tell you. I was just thinking that I used to be young and zealous for my King, just as you are. But I guess all that has changed now." He sighed.

"What has changed, sire? Do you not love His Majesty as you used to? Do you not rejoice to serve him, sire? Only recently did King Emmanuel adopt me—a year and a half ago, to be exact—but I have found that service to His Majesty is my greatest joy."

"My lord," the marquis said, with another great sigh, "I have served His Majesty for many years. No one has loved Emmanuel more, or served him more fervently, than I. And perhaps no one has paid a greater price to serve him than I."

"What do you mean, sire?"

"I lost my family, my lands, and my fortune because of my service to my King. There is no higher price to pay than that, my lord."

Josiah frowned. "How did it happen, Sir Dither?"

"I was on a quest for King Emmanuel when the enemy attacked my home. They destroyed my family and took my lands and my wealth. Had I not been away on service to my King, my men and I could have defended what was rightfully mine. After I completed the quest for Emmanuel, I returned home to find that everything I possessed had been taken from me. My men lost heart and deserted me at the time that I needed them the most. Aye, I have served Emmanuel, but it has cost me dearly."

"And now you've lost heart and are not sure that you want to continue serving His Majesty," Josiah said quietly, hoping that his words would not offend the marquis. "You've even entertained the thought that perhaps things would have been better had you served Argamor."

Sir Dither stiffened. "Do not say that, my lord."

"But isn't that what you have been thinking, sire?"

Sir Dither gave another great sigh. "Aye, to be honest, I have." He gestured toward the silent spellavision. "I watch the glowing images of houses and lands and wealth and beautiful women and magnificent horses, and... and I can't help but think that perhaps things would have been better had I served—" He dropped his head. "Nay, I cannot say that."

He was silent for a long moment, and then turned and looked into Josiah's eyes. "When I watch what is happening within the kingdom of Terrestria, it sometimes seems that Argamor is winning the battle and King Emmanuel is losing! To be quite honest, I've lost heart, lad. I am just not quite sure that it's worth it."

The marquis took a deep breath, shook his head, and gave a short laugh. "But why am I burdening you with all this? I don't even know you, and you are so young."

Josiah glanced upward and saw the white form of the dove perched in the rafters. He stepped to the window and looked down into the barbican below. "My story is quite the opposite of yours, sire. I have lost nothing, and gained everything. It wasn't that long ago that I was a slave to Argamor. I can still feel the chafing of the shackles on my ankle, feel the sting of his lash upon my back, and smell the rotting dungeon where I was imprisoned every night."

Terrifying memories overwhelmed him like a specter from the past as he told of the pain and suffering he had experienced at the hands of his cruel master, the hopelessness of his situation, the incredible loneliness. He described the despair that had flooded his soul when he tried to escape and found that he was helpless.

"And then King Emmanuel came and offered me freedom. Oh, the love that I saw in his eyes as he reached down with scarred hands and broke my shackles! Oh, the blessed freedom I experienced as my horrible chains fell away! That day, Emmanuel not only set me free, he adopted me as his own son. Never again can I go back to Argamor. I am eternally grateful to Emmanuel, and I rejoice to serve him. I long for the day when he returns from the Golden City and takes me to dwell with him."

Josiah turned back from the window, and as he did, was surprised to see that Sir Dither's eyes were filled with tears. "It was many, many years ago, my lord," the marquis said in a husky voice, "when His Majesty set me free. I suppose I have forgotten what servitude to Argamor was really like. Your words have touched my heart. I have no master but King Emmanuel, and I must once again serve him whole-heartedly."

He stepped over and touched the spellavision. "I sometimes wonder if this enchanting device has not been the source of my discontent."

Josiah nodded. "It has played a part, sire, of that I am certain. At Argamor's council of war the Council of Six laid out their strategies to steal the hearts of Emmanuel's subjects in order to wrest the kingdom away from Emmanuel. The spellavision played a prominent role in their plans."

Sir Dither's face tightened with resolution. "Look out the window, Prince Josiah. Is there anyone in the barbican below?"

Josiah peered out the window. "Not a soul, sire."

"Then stand back, my lord."

Josiah did, and the spellavision sailed out the window. Seconds later, a loud crash sounded in the barbican below. The young prince looked at the marquis in amazement.

"I thank you for coming, Prince Josiah. Your words have opened my eyes and touched my heart, and for that I am grateful. And now, if you'll excuse me, I need to be alone for awhile. I must send a petition to His Majesty."

An hour later, Josiah guided his horse around a huge rock formation and then descended into a quiet valley. He glanced upward to see a hawk gliding silently across the sky, and he immediately thought of the falcon he had caught for the marquis. "Thank you, Your Majesty," he said aloud, "for using me to be an encouragement to Sir Dither. I am grateful that you allow me to have a part in your kingdom."

He crossed the valley and entered a dense forest on the other side. The trees were close together here, and darkness closed in around him like a shroud. Feeling a bit uneasy, he urged the horse to a slightly faster pace. After a furlong or two, the trees thinned out and the forest became brighter, and he began to relax.

Through the trees just ahead he could make out a huge, indistinct shape, dark red in color. As he came to it he reined to a stop and sat staring. *The red rock spire of which the peasant spoke. I'm just three furlongs from the cottage and the egg!* His heart beat faster. He sat still, his mind racing. *It would take just a few moments to ride to the cottage, take a brief look at the egg, and then continue on my way. Surely a quick look will cause no harm.*

His mind made up, the young prince turned and rode north.

The peasant was drawing a bucket of water from the well as Josiah rode into the clearing. "Greetings, my lord," the peasant called, setting the bucket down and approaching the young prince's horse. "You have returned as planned."

Josiah was puzzled. "As planned, sir?"

The man shook his head. "Pay me no attention, my lord. It is good to see you again. Will you do me the honor of entering my humble abode?"

Josiah followed him into the cottage. "May I—may I see the egg again, sir? I was just riding by and thought I'd like to take another look—"

"Of course, my lord, of course," the peasant said agreeably, hurrying to open the large chest as he spoke. "It's no trouble at all." He carried the small brass chest to the table, opened it, and reached deep within. He gently lifted the alluring egg and held it out to Josiah. "Here. Hold it, my lord." The egg glowed as if a fire burned deep within its heart.

The young prince took the egg and felt a thrill of excitement as his fingers touched it. The egg was warm and soothing, and glowed even brighter as he held it, and he immediately began to desire it as never before. He longed to own it. Suddenly it seemed that nothing else in life really mattered; the only thing he wanted at that moment was to possess the magnificent egg.

"The egg is yours, my lord, with our gratitude." The elderly peasant placed his hands on Josiah's, pressing them against the egg. "We shall never forget what you and your friends did for us."

"I cannot—cannot accept it, sir, for my King has forbidden the possession of a dragon's egg." Josiah said the words, but his heart was not in them. He wanted the egg, desperately wanted the egg, and yet, at the same time he wanted to obey and honor King Emmanuel.

The peasant was looking at him strangely. "Do you know why King Emmanuel has forbidden the possession of dragon eggs within his kingdom?"

Josiah shook his head. "That I do not, sir."

"It's for your protection, my lord, and the protection of those around you. A dragon is a vicious beast, to be sure, and at times can be quite dangerous. A young Cararian Greatwing poses no threat to anyone, but an adult could be quite a menace. For this reason, His Majesty has outlawed the possession of eggs or dragons."

He touched the egg gently, almost reverently. "This egg, as my wife told you, has been in her family for generations. It is two hundred years old, at the very least, perhaps older. My lord, you need not worry that this egg will hatch. The little dragon inside this egg has been dead for nearly two centuries."

Josiah frowned. "The egg is dead? But it's warm... and it glows. And it... it feels alive."

The peasant laughed. "Of course it seems to glow, my lord. You are holding it in the sunlight from the window. The shell of the egg has a certain, uh, iridescence, and it reflects the light. It almost looks as if it is changing color, doesn't it? Here, move it away from the window. Watch what happens."

The young prince moved away from the window and held

the egg in a dark corner of the room. Immediately, the egg lost its luster. In the shadows, the magnificent egg seemed dull and lifeless.

"Do you see what I mean, my lord? The egg has been dormant for countless years. It poses no threat to anyone."

"But the King's law is still there," Josiah protested. "His Majesty has given orders that no one is to possess a dragon, nor the egg of a dragon."

The peasant sighed. "Aye, my lord, that is true, in a certain sense. But surely you would agree that His Majesty would not object to one owning an egg that has been dead for at least two centuries. Were the egg alive, you would do wrong to take it, and I would not offer it to you. Rather, I would crush it myself. But since there is no danger of it hatching, surely you can understand that it is permissible to have it. Would you not agree, my lord?"

Josiah hesitated. In his heart he knew that possession of the egg would be a violation of royal law, and yet, the peasant's words gave him an excuse—a way to justify his desire and silence his conscience.

"The peasant is attempting to deceive you, Prince Josiah," a quiet voice said. "Do not heed his words, for they are words of treachery and treason."

Josiah glanced over to see the dove sitting in the window, but the desire to possess the egg was so great that he chose to ignore the words of his celestial guide. "Are you certain that the egg cannot hatch, sir?"

"It had been dead for two centuries, my lord. It has no more chance of hatching than a rock."

The young prince sighed. In his heart he knew that he was about to break royal law. "I accept your gift, sir. I will take the egg."

Chapter Four

Daylight was fading rapidly as Prince Josiah rode across the drawbridge into the Castle of Faith. If he hurried he would be in time for the evening meal in the great hall. Reaching behind him, he felt the form of the egg in his saddlebag. His heart pounded and his chest tightened with apprehension. What if the egg were discovered? Taking a deep breath, he sat tall in the saddle, doing his best to look as if nothing were amiss.

"Josiah, my prince, how went the errand for Sir Faithful?" The young prince started at the sound of the booming voice as Sir Watchful, the castle constable, stepped forward to meet him. Sir Watchful was in charge of the castle's defenses.

Josiah gulped. "Things went well, sire," he replied. "I accomplished my purpose."

The constable nodded. "That is good to hear." He moved closer, staring intently at Josiah. "Are you all right? You look... troubled."

"I'm fine, sire," Josiah replied quickly. "Just a little tired." Sir Watchful smiled, nodded, and moved away.

"Your horse, my lord."

Josiah stared down at the young stable boy. "What?"

"I'm waiting for your horse, my lord. I'll take her to the stables."

"Oh." Josiah dismounted, handed the reins to the boy, and started up the stairs toward Sir Faithful's solar.

The egg! The stable boy would find it in his saddlebags! Josiah spun around just as the boy started away with the mare. "Wait!"

The boy turned. "Was there something else, my lord?"

Josiah took the stairs two at a time. "I—I just thought of an errand that I must run. I need my horse."

The boy handed him the reins. "The castle residents are gathering in the great hall for dinner, my lord."

"I know what time it is," Josiah snapped. "My dinner is none of your concern."

"Aye, my lord." The boy moved away with a hurt expression on his young face.

Josiah swung into the saddle and turned the mare toward the gate. Her hooves seemed unusually loud on the drawbridge as he rode swiftly out into the twilight. He rode along the edge of the moor, seeking a hiding place for the egg. *I must not keep it in my solar,* he decided, *lest someone find it there. There must be a place out here where no one will discover it.*

He found a hollow tree less than a furlong from the main gate of the castle. The tree was situated just inside the woods at the edge of the moor, but was out of sight of the castle gate. Dismounting, he reached into a large cavity in the trunk and carefully felt around in the darkness. The space was empty. The perfect hiding place! Glancing toward the castle to be certain that no one was coming, he retrieved the egg from his saddlebag, carried it across to the hollow tree, and carefully deposited it inside. He crouched in the darkness and scooped up several handfuls of dead grass and leaves, and then scattered them over the egg to help hide it. With a sigh of relief he swung into the saddle and galloped toward home.

Selwyn looked up as Josiah slid into his seat at the King's table. "You're later than I expected. Sir Faithful has already sent the petition of thanksgiving for the meal."

Josiah tried to catch his breath. "My errand took longer than I thought it would," he panted, hoping that he didn't look as guilty as he felt. His cheeks burned.

"How did the errand go? Weren't you on a mission for Sir Faithful?"

Josiah nodded. "It went well. Very well."

Gilda leaned across the table. "What was your errand?"

He shook his head. "Sir Faithful told me not to discuss it."

"Oh." A look of disappointment swept across the princess' pretty face.

A procession of attendants filed by just then, bearing platters of miniature meat pastries, pheasant in cinnamon sauce, beef fritters, eels in spicy puree, loaches in cold green sauce, slices of roast mutton, filets of saltwater fish, and various garden vegetables. Josiah took some of each, nearly filling his trencher. An attendant approached with a huge silver platter, on which was fruit jelly sculpted into the form of a crown. Josiah waved the attendant away.

"We eat well at His Majesty's table, don't we?" Selwyn commented.

Josiah reached in with both hands and began to eat, enjoying the rich and unusual delicacies of the royal feast. The flaky pastries filled with tender venison, the hot, spicy fritters, the steaming vegetables smothered in butter, the succulent slices of mutton—it was indeed a feast fit for a king, and Josiah was enjoying every morsel. A minstrel strolled among the tables, strumming his lute and singing ballads that told of the greatness of King Emmanuel.

The second song was one that Josiah did not care to hear that night:

"I sing the greatness of my King, my Lord Emmanuel
His power is great and far exceeds
What mortal tongue or pen can tell.
My heart is full; I sing for him,
And trust that I may serve him well."

The song was Josiah's favorite, one he had heard on his very first night in the Castle of Faith, but tonight it only served to remind him of his disobedience. Usually an anthem of joy, tonight it was a source of torment. He groaned inwardly as the minstrel started on the second stanza:

"I sing the love of my great King, my Lord Emmanuel
His lovingkindness ransomed me,
But why he did, I cannot tell.
His love led him to die for me,
I trust that I may serve him well."

The song went on to tell of the horrible dungeon of sin in which the minstrel had once been imprisoned, the pain and agony of servitude to sin, and how the gracious hand of King Emmanuel had reached down and set him free. Listening to the story presented in song, Josiah struggled with his emotions. *Have I betrayed my King, the one who set me free?* He pushed the thought from his mind.

Josiah idly touched the golden ring upon his hand, unconsciously using his fingertip to trace the design of the King's coat of arms in the center of the magnificent sapphire. He sat back with a sigh, suddenly unable to eat. Tonight there was no thrill of joy at the warmth of the crackling fire upon the hearth, the exquisite food, the cheerful, loving companionship of those about him, and the beautiful music praising his King. Tonight there was a cold, dark void within his soul.

At last, the meal was finished. Josiah hurried from the great hall, not wanting to speak to anyone, but knowing that he would have to give a report to Sir Faithful. He dreaded the meeting—the old castle steward, his mentor and close friend, seemed at times to have the ability to see right through him. What would he say tonight?

"Josiah, wait for us!" Josiah turned at the sound of Gilda's voice. "Josiah, where are you hurrying off to? You left the table like a warhorse charging into battle!"

The young prince shrugged. "Sorry. I have to report to Sir Faithful."

"Sir Faithful is still in the great hall," Selwyn said quietly.

Josiah didn't answer.

"So tell me about your mission," Sir Faithful said moments later as Josiah followed him into the steward's solar. The old man's eyes twinkled. "When I gave you this assignment, you told me that you were too young for a mission such as this. You doubted that a nobleman like Sir Dither would even listen to you. Did he?"

Josiah took a seat before the fireplace where a cheerful fire crackled on the hearth. "The mission was a success, sire," he replied. "Sir Dither's heart is now surrendered to Emmanuel's will, though it wasn't when I first met him."

"So he did listen to you, I assume?"

"Aye, he listened very well, sire, though I am quite young. Of course, the falcon helped with that, I suppose."

"The falcon?"

"Sir Dither is an avid falconer, and one of his newest falcons got loose. I was waiting in the bailey for the noon meal, and she happened to land close to where I was sitting. I caught her for him. When we took the falcon back to his solar to return her to her cage, we had a chance to talk. He bared his heart to me."

"You say that his heart was not surrendered at first?"

"I believe he was discouraged, sire, and had lost sight of what King Emmanuel had done for him. He told me that it sometimes seems that Argamor is winning the battle for the kingdom, and that Emmanuel is losing. His heart was no longer dedicated to the service of our King, and he had become discouraged in the battle." He stared into the fire. "The spellavision had something to do with it, I dare say."

The old steward nodded. "Argamor has begun to use the spellavision quite effectively to draw men's hearts away from their rightful King."

"Anyway, before I left his solar, he had decided that he wanted to serve King Emmanuel whole-heartedly again. He was preparing to send a petition to Emmanuel when I left him."

"Excellent, Prince Josiah, excellent!" the old man exclaimed, striding across the chamber to lay a hand on the young prince's shoulder. "You have done well."

"I did not do it, sire, for I had no idea what to say to Sir Dither. The dove was present, and I believe that he guided my words."

Sir Faithful beamed. "I am delighted to hear you say that, my prince, for it shows your realization of your need to depend on him. Tell me—exactly what did you say to Sir Dither?"

Josiah thought for a moment. "I suppose that I just told him the story of the day that King Emmanuel rescued me from Argamor," he said quietly. "I told him that I was thrilled to be a child of Emmanuel, and thrilled to be in his service. The next thing I knew, the marquis was weeping and telling me that he wanted to serve King Emmanuel with all his heart again."

"His Majesty used you in a great way today, my prince," Sir Faithful said softly, "because your heart is yielded to his will. Had you attempted this mission in your own strength, you would have met with failure."

Josiah nodded, but said nothing. *What would Sir Faithful say if he knew about the egg?* he thought miserably. *My heart is no longer yielded to Emmanuel.*

Sir Faithful's clear blue eyes seemed to be looking right through him. "What are you thinking, my prince? Your thoughts are troubled."

Josiah shook his head. "I'm just tired, sire. This has been a long day."

Sir Faithful studied his face for a long moment without saying a word. Josiah felt uncomfortable. "Get some sleep, Josiah," the old steward said at last. "This day you have served your King well."

Josiah's heart was in turmoil as he said good night to the steward and walked up to his own solar.

Silver moonbeams danced upon the floor of Josiah's solar, almost as bright as the rays of sunshine that usually splashed through his window in the daytime. An owl hooted in the distance, and Josiah shivered as he drew the coverlet up to his chin. Tonight he felt so alone, so... distant. He thought of King Emmanuel and the Golden City, but tonight they seemed so far away, so unreachable. He groaned inwardly. He had gotten in the habit of sending a petition of thanksgiving and worship to King Emmanuel each night before going to bed, but this time he had forgotten. He sighed as he admitted to himself that he had no desire to even send one.

It was the egg's fault. That cursed egg, so colorful and warm and inviting, had somehow separated him from the one who loved him most. *Tomorrow at first light I shall go out on the moor, find the egg, and take it back to the peasant who gave it to me,* he promised himself. *Then it shall be his worry, not mine. Possessing the egg is not worth the loneliness and emptiness I feel inside.*

"It is the egg of a Cararian Greatwing," a voice within him seemed to say, "and no one else in all of Terrestria has one. Enjoy it for awhile; you can always take it back later. No one but the peasant in the forest knows that you have it, so it can bring no trouble. Enjoy the ownership of the egg for a few days and then take it back."

He thought about the egg itself. "A rare jewel," the peasant had called it, and the term was fitting. The egg was so beautiful, so warm, so alluring. Just looking at it brought mysterious feelings of pleasure and wonderment, and touching it increased those sensations. Ownership of the egg brought an even greater thrill. True, ownership of any dragon's egg was a transgression of royal law, but after all, this egg was dead, and so, in reality, it was not the same at all. The King's edict against dragon's eggs applied only to the live ones, though the wording of the law did not specifically say so.

He sighed again. He would just keep the egg for a day or two, and then take it back. His eyelids grew heavy and he could no longer keep his eyes open.

He sensed rather than heard a slight noise, and his eyes flew open. Someone had quietly closed the door to his solar, meaning that someone had also opened it. He lay still, holding his breath, moving only his eyes as he surveyed the room.

The moonbeams still danced upon the floor like spirits from another world, but the solar was empty. Perhaps his imagination was playing tricks on him.

He gasped as he saw the barest trace of movement at the foot of his bed. A human figure, not clearly visible, had taken a step toward him. He lay still, afraid to move, afraid to call out, afraid to breathe. He stared, but could see nothing.

The apparition slowly materialized, a tall, slender woman of white, arrayed in a long, flowing gown of white. The lady had a pleasant, friendly face, softly framed by long, golden hair. Her pearl-white gown fluttered gently in the breeze from the open window. In her left hand she held a single rose, a deep crimson blossom that glowed with a light all its own, and with her right hand she was slowly plucking the petals and dropping them to the floor.

Josiah gave a sigh of relief. "Lady Prudence!" He sat up in bed.

The woman, so gossamer and transparent that he could still see the wall behind her, was moving silently toward the bed. At last, she spoke. "Prince Josiah," she whispered softly, and her voice was the gentle sound of a summer breeze, "I have come to deliver a warning. The dragon's egg can bring you nothing but sorrow. Crush it, my prince, before it crushes you."

She moved closer, still dropping crimson rose petals.

"Drag—dragon's egg, my lady?" Josiah's voice came out as a squeak. "Of what d-dragon's egg do you speak?"

"The egg lies hidden in the heart of an oak at the edge of the moor," Lady Prudence said softly, "though in reality, you have hidden it from no one."

"H—how did you know about t-the egg?" Josiah was trembling.

"The entire castle shall soon know, my prince," the lady said, with a gentle laugh. "Sir Faithful shall know. Prince Selwyn and Princess Gilda shall know. The egg is not as well hidden as you might think."

Josiah sat rigid, uncertain as to what to say or do. He felt no fear at the white lady's appearance; but an overwhelming sense of shame engulfed him as he realized that the ethereal visitor knew of the dragon's egg. At last, he rose slowly to his feet. "What am I to do, my lady?"

"You have made a foolish choice today, my prince. You must alter that choice. Tonight I want you to make another visit to the Lake of Destiny."

"The Lake of Destiny, my lady? But that is so far away!"

"Aye," she replied quietly, "but not as far as you would think, for I have arranged the journey for you. The Lake of Destiny can show you the possible consequences of the choice that you have made today, in order that you might alter that choice before it is too late. Prince Josiah, if there is within your heart the least desire to please your King, take this brief journey. Go with an open heart that you may make your choice wisely."

"How am I to find the Lake of Destiny, my lady? It is so far from the castle."

Lady Prudence opened the door of Josiah's solar. "I have arranged that," she replied, stepping out onto the sentry walk. Josiah followed her.

Raising her hand to her mouth, the ethereal visitor gave a loud, shrill whistle. At once, the sound of distant thunder reverberated across the starry heavens, and the young prince knew immediately what it was. "The lepidopteras," he said softly.

As he watched, a golden creature resembling a giant butterfly with enormous, colorful wings dropped from the darkness of the night. Its shimmering, transparent wings beat rapidly as it hovered above the castle, flashing dazzling rainbows of color and light across the darkness of the heavens. As the lepidoptera dropped slowly toward the earth to land within the bailey of the castle, the downdrafts from the gigantic wings made the branches of the trees within the bailey dance and gyrate as if they were being pounded by a violent windstorm.

Prince Josiah felt a sense of awe, although he and Selwyn and Gilda had seen and ridden the incredible creatures before. *Just like Gilda said,* he thought, thoroughly fascinated, *wings that look like enormous stained glass windows.*

"The lepidoptera will take you to the Lake of Destiny," Lady Prudence told him. She was starting to fade from view. "Go with an open heart, my prince." With those words she vanished, leaving Josiah to stare into the empty darkness of the night.

Josiah hurried down the stairs. Reaching the bailey, he dashed across the lawn toward the waiting lepidoptera. He hesitated just for an instant and then climbed up on the enormous back. He crawled forward and sat on the thorax of the huge creature. Wrapping his legs around the lepidoptera's middle, he leaned forward and grasped the powerful muscles attaching the massive wings to the body.

The huge wings immediately began to beat rapidly and the lepidoptera lifted majestically into the air. The young prince felt a breathtaking surge of fear and excitement. Looking down, he saw that already he was nearly a hundred feet above the castle.

Within minutes the huge butterfly had reached the Lake of Destiny and landed gently on the sandy shore. As Josiah crawled down from the unusual means of transport he glanced toward the lake, noting with delight that the moon had created a shimmering, silvery path across the surface of the water. "The Lake of Destiny," he said aloud. Legend claimed that a man could explore his own future by visiting the lake, and the young prince had found out for himself on a previous visit that there was truth to the legend.

A loon called from across the lake, and Josiah shivered. The loon's call was so lonely... so mournful. He stared out at the shimmering water. Why did Lady Prudence want him to visit the lake again? Hearing a slight whisper of a noise, he turned and found Lady Prudence waiting for him.

The woman moved silently toward the water. Josiah found himself compelled to follow. She paused at the water's edge, standing at the very point where the shimmering path began. "Follow the silver path, Prince Josiah. As before, you need not fear the water; the lake itself will take you into the realm of what lies ahead in order that you might learn and profit."

Josiah stepped to the water's edge. He hesitated for the tiniest moment and then stepped into the shimmering silver path on the moonlit waters. At once he felt two overwhelming sensations—the thrill of eager anticipation, and, at the same time, a deep and settled peace.

Chapter Five

Prince Josiah's heart was pounding furiously as he waded out into the rippling waters of the Lake of Destiny. The water swirled around his knees, but there was no sensation of cold wetness. He waded deeper. When the water reached his waist, he paused in a moment of uncertainty, but Lady Prudence called to him reassuringly. "Do not fear, Prince Josiah. You are about to view the future again. If your heart is open, my prince, this night will help you make a right decision."

Josiah stepped forward. The water grew deeper. He felt a moment of panic when the waters closed about his shoulders, but he pushed resolutely forward. Still he felt no sensation of cold water around his body. It seemed that the waters of the lake had no substance, as if they weren't really there. *Perhaps this is indeed an enchanted lake,* he thought, strangely detached and unconcerned as he walked deeper.

He looked up to notice a shimmering, silvery ceiling just above his head and knew that he was looking up at the surface of the lake. He was submerged beneath the water. He had already passed beneath the surface of the lake, and yet, still he could breathe.

Josiah saw a sudden flash of light. For just an instant, he felt dizzy and nauseous, and he closed his eyes. He opened them to discover that his environs had changed. Shading his eyes against the sudden brightness that surrounded him, he looked around. He was standing on the bank of a wide river in broad daylight. Judging from the position of the sun, he estimated that it was late afternoon. He glanced upward and saw that the shimmering ceiling had disappeared. He had stepped through a doorway into another world.

Josiah glanced across toward the far shore of the river and his heart leaped. Situated just beyond the river was a glistening city whose walls appeared to be built of solid gold. The city gleamed with a light that rivaled that of the sun. He was seeing the Golden City. It was the most majestic, most beautiful sight that he had ever seen. "The City of the Redeemed," he said quietly. His heart was filled with wonder.

He was startled to realize that his right hand was resting on the large wooden wheel of an oxcart. The vehicle was heavily loaded with packages of various sizes and shapes, and he knew instinctively that the oxcart belonged to him. With a trembling hand, he led the oxen forward. He took a deep breath and stepped into the water.

When the oxcart reached deeper water, it began to float. Soon the oxen were swimming. Josiah pushed ahead resolutely. The water never reached his shoulders. The young prince was surprised at how easily he made the crossing.

As Josiah stepped from the water on the opposite shore, a regal figure moved from the gate of the city and hurried to meet him. Josiah's heart leaped. King Emmanuel! The gracious King greeted the young prince warmly. "Welcome home, my son! Welcome to the Golden City of the Redeemed. We have anxiously awaited your arrival."

Josiah fell to his knees at King Emmanuel's feet. "My Lord!"

"The Golden City is your eternal home," the monarch said quietly. "Welcome home."

Josiah rose to his feet. He gestured toward the heavily loaded cart where the two oxen waited patiently. "Here is what I have to present, Your Majesty." He lowered his head.

"We will see if it passes the test," King Emmanuel said. At a gesture from his hand, two bright beings in shimmering robes hurried forward with flaming torches. As Josiah watched in disbelief, they unhitched the oxen, led them away a short distance, and then set fire to the oxcart and its contents. Soon the flames were leaping so high that Josiah could see their flickering reflection on the golden walls of the city.

As the fire burned down, Josiah was amazed to see that there was nothing left of the oxcart and its load but a small, smoldering pile of ashes. In the center of the ash pile rested a large, blackened egg. The young prince stared in dismay at the smoking heap. King Emmanuel stepped toward him. "Have you nothing to present to me, my son? Each day of your life was an opportunity to lay up treasures for the Golden City, but you have brought nothing but ashes. As my son, you are welcome in the city, but have you nothing to offer me?"

"Nay, my Lord." Josiah bowed his head, tears coursing down his cheeks, as he stood empty-handed before his King. "I have nothing to offer."

Josiah turned away. What a disappointment, what a heartbreak, to finally reach the Golden City of the Redeemed and stand before King Emmanuel with nothing to offer! The sun dropped behind the hills just then, plunging the riverbank into abrupt darkness. Josiah turned back toward the Golden City and saw that it was still ablaze with light.

The young prince abruptly found himself on the opposite bank of the river, across from the Golden City. He turned and retraced his steps. Moments later, as he followed the road up a gentle slope, he looked up to see the shimmering silver surface just above his head. He climbed higher, and abruptly broke through the surface to find himself emerging from the Lake of Destiny. He opened his eyes, and to his amazement discovered that he was lying in his own bed in the Castle of Faith.

He leaned over the side of the bed, carefully searching the moonlit floor. There were no rose petals to be found—Lady Prudence had not visited him, after all—and he realized that the entire adventure had been just a dream. He gave a sigh of relief. His secret was safe, then—no one knew about the dragon's egg.

"Lord Watchful is giving an exhibition of swordsmanship this afternoon," Prince Selwyn told Josiah as they walked out of the great hall after the noon meal. "It's to be held in the east bailey."

Josiah nodded. "I know."

"Are you coming?" Gilda asked.

Josiah shrugged indifferently. "I think I'll take a walk instead."

"Lord Watchful is said to be one of the best, if not the best, swordsman in all of Terrestria," Selwyn reminded him. "We could pick up some important tips."

"I still think I'll just walk."

"Want some company?"

"I'd rather be alone."

His friend tilted his head to one side and looked at him curiously. "Are you all right, Josiah? You were awfully quiet at dinner. Is something wrong?"

Josiah shook his head. "I'm fine. I just need some time alone—a chance to think through some things."

Selwyn nodded to show that he understood. "Enjoy the walk. Gilda and I are heading for the exhibition."

"Enjoy the exhibition. I'll see you later." Josiah turned and headed for the main castle gate.

"Where's your horse, my lord?" a sentry greeted him as he entered the gatehouse afoot. "You didn't wear her out yesterday, did you?"

The young prince laughed just to be polite. "I'm just out for a walk. I won't go far enough to need a horse."

He crossed the drawbridge and followed the winding lane down to the bottom of the hill. At the edge of the moor he glanced around to be certain that no one was watching and then slipped into the woods that bordered the road. Moments later he came to the hollow tree. His heart pounded as he stood quietly for a moment, watching, listening. Glancing furtively around, he approached the hollow oak.

Josiah reached into the cavity inside the tree. He felt a thrill of excitement as his fingers touched the egg. He lifted it carefully from its hiding place, cradling it in his arms like a baby. The egg began to glow, first with a soft golden color and then gradually changing to a deep blue. The young prince stared at it in alarm. The peasant had told him that the egg was dead, but what if it was still alive? What if there was a little dragon inside, just waiting for the opportunity to hatch? Just how dangerous would a hatchling Cararian Greatwing be?

"He came this way," a voice said suddenly. "I know he's in these woods somewhere."

Josiah's heart leaped into his throat. Someone was coming! In a panic, he hurriedly thrust the egg back into its hiding place. Dropping to the ground, he crawled into a dense thicket.

A branch broke with a snap and two knights from the Castle of Faith strode into view. Both carried crossbows. The men paused at the base of the oak. "Search for him," one man ordered. "He couldn't have gone far." Josiah recognized the voice as that of Lord Integrity, an earl known for his loyalty to Emmanuel.

"I'll drop him with one shot when we find him," the other declared.

In his hiding place not more than eight feet away, Josiah trembled uncontrollably. His chest constricted with fear, and sweat broke out on his forehead. Why were these men searching for him?

"Our orders are to bring him back alive so that he may stand before Lord Severity for judgment," Lord Integrity replied sternly. "Let's have no more talk of killing him. We won't take his life unless it's absolutely necessary."

"Wait here," a third voice ordered, and Josiah cringed as he realized that there were other knights present. "My men will search the woods and the moor." *A whole garrison of knights from another castle,* Josiah thought frantically. *I don't stand a chance!*

Josiah flattened his face against the ground and lay as still as possible. His heart pounded so vigorously that he was certain that the men would hear it and discover his hiding place. He heard the crackling of brush and voices calling to each other as the garrison of knights searched the woods and the moors. Lord Integrity moved closer, pausing just a step or two from Josiah's face. The young prince cowered in fear. *Why did I ever accept the egg?* he berated himself. *I'm about to be discovered, and that will bring disgrace to me and to the name of King Emmanuel. If only I had never gone back for a second look. I thought it would be harmless, but down in my heart I should have known what would happen.*

I'll take it back, he vowed silently. *If I make it out of this, I'll take the egg back to the peasant and demand that he take it back. I will not keep it one day longer.*

"Here are his tracks!" a voice called. "We have him now."

Josiah cringed. It was only a matter of time before his hiding place would be discovered. The tracks would lead the solders right to him. Perhaps it would go easier with him if he simply gave himself up.

Lord Integrity took another step backward, crushing one of the branches of the bush under which the young prince was hidden. He was standing so close that the heel of his saboton was less than eighteen inches from Josiah's face. Josiah tried to breathe as shallowly as possible.

He felt a stinging sensation on his elbow and turned his eyes in that direction. Ants! A solid line of large, red ants were making their way through the grass, across his arm, and back down a gnarled root. He dared not move, dared not brush them away. The slightest movement would betray him to Sir Integrity, who towered over him. He bit his lip as one of the insects sank its stinger into his flesh. How much more of this torment could he take?

The sensation of the myriad ants crawling on his bare arm was almost more than he could bear. He longed to leap to his feet, to cry out, to slap the torturous insects from his body. He forced himself to lie still, but he trembled with the effort.

"We have you!" a voice cried triumphantly. "Give yourself up before we fill your carcass with shafts of steel."

Josiah let out his breath in a long sigh. It was over. They had found him.

"Stand to your feet slowly," a harsh voice ordered. "My men have orders to shoot if you try to escape."

"I yield! I yield!" a terrified voice cried. "I am yours. I will not try to escape." To Josiah's amazement, a man crawled from a thicket and stood to his feet less than twenty feet from Josiah's hiding place. Two knights stepped forward and clamped irons on him.

"With what crime is the blackguard charged?" one of the knights asked.

"He's an agent for Argamor," another voice replied. "He attempted to poison the well at the Castle of Virtue. We endeavored to capture him within the castle, but he managed to elude us until now. An entire garrison has been on his trail for three days."

The fugitive was led away with his head down, and the garrison of knights from the Castle of Virtue went with him. Within moments, a hush had settled over the woods. Josiah let out a sigh of relief. He crawled from the thicket, stood to his feet, and began vigorously brushing ants from his arms and neck.

"Prince Josiah!" Sir Integrity exclaimed in amazement. "What were you doing under there?"

"Aargh!" Josiah nearly jumped out of his doublet. His heart skipped a beat. "You scared me, sire. I didn't know that you were still here."

The earl laughed. "Well, you startled me, my prince, crawling out of the bushes like that. Whatever were you doing in that thicket?"

Josiah couldn't think of an appropriate answer, so he simply turned and walked away. His face burned with embarrassment. Sir Integrity stood staring after him.

The afternoon sun beat upon Prince Josiah's back as he rode over the crest of the hill. Just a few more furlongs and he would arrive at the peasant's cottage. He reached behind the saddle and touched the bulge in his saddlebags. In just a few moments he would be free of the troublesome dragon's egg. As yet no one knew that he had it, but he wasn't sure how much longer he could avoid discovery.

"My guilty conscience just won't leave me alone," he told his horse. "I had trouble sleeping last night, and I still can't get the dream out of my mind about the trip through the Lake of Destiny. And after what happened just a little while ago in the woods, I've decided that possession of the egg just isn't worth it."

The mare forded a shallow stream. Fifty yards downstream, a family of raccoons—a father, mother, and two half-grown kits—frolicked in the water as they hunted for fresh-water mussels, but Josiah didn't see them. The black-masked creatures paused and looked up in curiosity as he passed, and then went back to their hunting and playing.

The young prince looked up to see the red rock spire towering over him, some eighty or ninety feet high. "We're almost there," he told the mare. "Three furlongs north and we find the peasant's cabin. And then I'm free of this wretched egg."

Moments later he entered the familiar clearing. He reined to a stop and sat silently, staring in astonishment. The peasant's cottage was gone. There was no well, no cottage, nothing to show that any dwelling had ever existed. All had vanished without a trace.

Chapter Six

Josiah dismounted and walked slowly across the clearing, studying the ground as he went. "Here's where we left the horses," he said aloud, kneeling to examine three sets of hoof prints in the soil. He traced the outline of a print with his finger. "I'd recognize the mare's tracks anywhere."

He stood and walked methodically across the clearing. "And here's where I came back for the egg. This is the same clearing—it has to be! But where is the cottage? And how could a well just disappear?"

Puzzled, he crossed and re-crossed the clearing repeatedly, searching for any sign of the cottage. But other than the prints of the horses, the ground was bare, devoid of any sign that the cottage or well had ever existed. He turned about in a slow circle, studying the trees, noticing the path that led from the forest. There was absolutely no doubt in his mind: this was the same clearing.

"Now what shall I do with the egg?' he asked aloud, though he expected no answer. "I shall not take it back to the castle; I have no other choice but to just leave it here."

Josiah opened his saddlebags and carefully removed the dragon's egg. He cradled it in his hands for a moment, noticing again that the egg, gray and dull when he brought it out, was now beginning to glow and pulse with color. To his chagrin, it felt warm and alive. *What if the peasant lied to me?* he wondered. *What if the egg really is alive and can still hatch?* The idea frightened him.

He squared his shoulders, resolute and determined. Carrying the egg to the edge of the forest, he carefully placed it on the ground, situating it between two tree roots so that it could not roll. "I want you, want you desperately," he told the egg, "but my Lord King Emmanuel has decreed that his subjects shall not possess the egg of a dragon. I cannot keep you."

He looked at the egg one last time and then steeled himself to turn and walk away. The egg, now golden in color, pulsated and shimmered with iridescent highlights. The shimmering surface seemed to throb with a familiar rhythm, glowing and pulsating with iridescent light and all the colors of the rainbow. The young prince watched, fascinated, as the egg once again mimicked the rhythm of his own heart.

"Never!" he cried aloud, as if to reinforce his own determination. "This is the egg of a dragon! My Lord King Emmanuel has forbidden me to have it. The egg stays here." Clenching his fists, he forced himself to turn his back on the egg and return to his horse.

With a sigh of relief, he mounted. "It's as if the egg is calling to me," he told the mare, "and I must not listen. I must never listen! I am determined to leave it here once and for all. We must return to the Castle of Faith without it." With a shake of the reins, he rode from the clearing.

He made the mistake of glancing over his shoulder for one last look at the egg. A tiny little imp of a man dressed in a green jerkin and brown leggings was standing on the tree root and staring at the egg. The little man was slightly less than a foot tall, with spindly legs and arms and a curly, brown beard. Josiah quickly reined to a stop. At that moment, another tiny man dressed in a blue jerkin and black leggings joined the first.

Josiah caught his breath. Littlekins! He had met up with the tiny folk before. While on a quest to seven castles for King Emmanuel, the Littlekins had captured him and taken him to their village to be tried before a diminutive magistrate known as Lord Careless. Josiah recognized the little man in green as Envy, the Littlekin who had gotten him into trouble.

He quietly led the mare behind a tree, tied her, and then crept through the woods toward the two tiny men. "It will take a farm wagon to carry it back to the village," Envy was saying. "Why don't you go back into town for a wagon? I'll stay here and guard the egg."

"Nay, I shall stay and guard the egg while you go for the wagon," his companion argued.

"Discontent, listen to me. I found the egg, so I will stay and guard it. You fetch the wagon."

"I am a better swordsman than you," Discontent retorted, "so I shall remain to guard the egg. You shall fetch the wagon."

Envy snorted in derision. "You? A better swordsman than I? Surely you jest, knave."

"I'll match steel with you any time you're ready," the tiny man in blue replied hotly. "I'm your better, and you know it. Now, fetch the wagon while I stand guard."

"You're not even wearing your sword, you pompous little puff of wind," Envy countered. "I found the egg, so I will guard it. Now, make haste and bring the wagon."

Envy and Discontent argued and argued while Josiah listened in amusement to their angry exchanges. When it seemed that they were about to come to blows, he stepped from behind the tree. "There will be no need to fetch a wagon, little men," he said, mockingly. "The egg is mine. I am taking it back to my castle."

Envy screamed with rage. "Liar! We found the egg, and you have no claim to it! Stand back, you over-sized buffoon! The egg belongs to us, and you shall not touch it."

Josiah laughed scornfully. He leaned down and placed one finger against the little man's chest, knocking him over backwards. Envy scrambled to his feet, hopping up and down in fury. "You have no claim to the egg!" he screamed in a voice shrill with rage. "Do not touch it! I found it first and I claim it for the village!"

"The egg was given to me by the rightful owners, who have had it in their family for generations," the young prince replied contemptuously. "You did not find it, for it already belongs to me. I left it here under the tree and I have come back to reclaim it." Josiah reached for the egg.

"I say again, the egg is ours and you are to leave it alone," the furious Littlekin asserted, leaping in front of the egg with his arms folded across his tiny chest in a gesture of defiance. Discontent joined him, glaring furiously up at Josiah.

The young prince laughed and easily pushed the tiny men to one side. "Move out of the way, Littlekins. The egg is mine."

A look of terror crossed Discontent's face. He leaped backwards, pointing skyward and screaming, "Beware of the falling branch!"

Josiah leaped backwards and rolled to one side in a valiant attempt to escape the danger of the falling limb. He landed sprawling in the grass. Raising himself to his knees, he looked for the fallen branch, but there was none. "There's no cause for alarm," he chided the Littlekin. "No branch is—"

He stopped in mid-sentence, staring at the spot where the dragon's egg had rested. The egg and the Littlekins were gone. He leaped to his feet.

The dragon's egg was making its way through the brush

beyond the tree. He darted forward. Grunting with the effort, the two tiny men were carrying the egg, moving as fast as their little legs could go. "Oh, no, you don't!" Josiah cried, reaching down for the egg.

He was too late. The dragon's egg dropped out of sight.

Josiah fell to his knees and lunged forward, parting the weeds with his hands. To his dismay, he found that the Littlekins had managed to push the precious egg into a badger's hole. He dropped to his belly in the weeds and peered into the darkness of the burrow.

The hole angled down for eight or ten inches, and then leveled out into a horizontal tunnel. Four feet into the burrow, the two tiny men stood in front of the egg, laughing at him. "The egg is ours, buffoon," Envy taunted. "Try to take it from us now."

Josiah reached into the burrow as far as he could, but could feel nothing. The Littlekins and the egg were just out of reach. He gritted his teeth in frustration. As small as the Littlekins were, he was powerless to take the dragon's egg from them.

"I'll get you when you come out," he raged, cupping his hands to his mouth and shouting into the hole in an effort to intimidate his tiny adversaries. "You cannot stay in there forever. When I get my hands on you, I'll squash you like ticks. Now give me the egg."

"Words are worthless, big one," Discontent jeered. "You have your words but we have the egg."

Trembling with rage, Josiah found a dead branch and carried it back to the badger den. He thrust it into the hole as far as he could reach, but felt nothing. Taunts and laughter rewarded his efforts. Removing the branch, he knelt and peered into the tunnel. The Littlekins had moved the dragon's egg safely out of reach.

"Keep the egg!" he shouted into the hole. "I'm returning to the castle. But the next time I see you, I'll squash you both like bugs." He walked across to his horse, mounted, and rode from the clearing to give the impression that he was leaving. A hundred yards from the tree, he stopped, tied the mare to a sturdy sapling, and quietly crept back to the entrance of the burrow. Noiselessly, he sank to a sitting position in the weeds.

I'll wait here until they think I'm gone, he told himself with gleeful satisfaction, *and then grab them when they bring the egg out. No wretched Littlekins are going to outsmart me!*

Half an hour later, he was still waiting. He had heard nothing from the two tiny men in the burrow. At last, impatient to be on his way, he leaned down and peered into the hole. The tunnel was empty; the Littlekins and the egg were gone. He stared, unable to believe his eyes. *That's impossible,* he thought. *They could not have taken the egg from the burrow without me seeing them. I've been right here the whole time.*

Peering into the darkness of the burrow for a second time, he spotted a coin-sized circle of light and realized that he was seeing daylight. The burrow had a second entrance! He leaped to his feet and raced to the other end of the burrow. He groaned as he found the second entrance. Tiny footprints and trampled grass confirmed what he had suspected: Envy and Discontent had pushed the egg out through the second entrance. Tiny footprints and a parallel set of wagon wheel tracks six inches apart led from the opening and disappeared into the brush. A tiny wagon had carted the precious egg away.

He stood slowly to his feet. Outwitted by the Littlekins! The shame of it raged throughout his being, frustrating and angering him. "The egg is mine," he growled softly, "and no Littlekin is going to take it from me. I'll do whatever it takes to get it back."

The wagon tracks! They would lead him to the Littlekins, and to the egg!

Dropping to his knees in the grass, he began to follow the tracks left by the passing of the miniature wagon. The tracks led through a dense thicket—which was painful going for Josiah—and down a gentle slope. The young prince crawled on hands and knees as he hunted for the little men and the wagon. When he reached the edge of a trickle of water that was too small to properly be called a stream, he lost the tracks entirely. It was as if the wagon had disappeared into thin air.

Finally, after searching for several anxious moments, he picked up the trail again when the tracks crossed a bare patch of sandy soil. He followed them around a huge boulder, and, to his surprise, found the wagon.

The tiny wagon was parked in the shade of the boulder. Hitched to the wagon was a yearling rabbit. The egg rested in the back of the wagon, completely filling the bed. Envy and Discontent sat side by side on the narrow seat, totally unaware of Josiah's presence. "We can't just come driving into the village with it," Discontent was saying. "The others would try to take it from us."

"Let's leave the wagon here until we have talked with Lord Careless," Envy replied. "Once we have made proper claim to the egg, we can safely bring it into town and no one will dare try to seize it."

"One of us should stand guard."

"Perhaps," Envy replied. "Why don't you stand guard while I go file a claim with Lord Careless?"

"Hardly!" the other snorted. "Do you think I'm going to stay here while you lay claim to the egg? I know you, Envy. You'll file in your own name and leave me out." He looked slyly at his companion. "I'll go and you stay."

"Buttermilk!" Envy retorted angrily. "Do you take me for a

fool? I'm not about to let you lay claim to the egg while I stay here with the wagon."

"Then I'd venture to say that we are at a stalemate, since neither of us will trust the other. Who will go and lay claim to the egg?"

The Littlekins sat in silence as they pondered the problem. After several minutes, Envy brightened. "We'll both go!"

Discontent frowned. "And leave the egg here?"

Prince Josiah stepped around the edge of the boulder. "Why don't I stay and guard the egg while you both go," he said, triumphantly, laughing when both Littlekins jumped with fright at the sound of his voice. "The dragon's egg is mine, little men. Thank you for guarding it for me." He reached for the egg.

"Hi-Yee!" Envy cracked his tiny whip, and the rabbit leaped forward. The wagon bounced over the rough sod, taking the egg with it.

"Oh, no you don't!" Josiah cried. Leaping forward, he caught the wagon and jerked it to a standstill. Envy and Discontent were catapulted from the wagon seat and tumbled head over heels. The rabbit crouched, trembling with fear.

Josiah retrieved the dragon's egg from the wagon. Envy scrambled to his feet. "Thief! Leave the egg where it is, I say!"

In reply, the young prince drew back his foot and kicked with all his might, snapping the traces and splintering the wagon into a thousand pieces. The rabbit, now free, dashed for cover. The Littlekins howled with rage.

Clutching the precious egg to his bosom, Josiah hurried to his horse. A deep sense of satisfaction flooded his being. He had bested the little men after all, and the dragon's egg was his again. He would not have been so pleased with himself had he realized that he had just walked into a trap cleverly set by two of Argamor's most capable agents.

Chapter Seven

Prince Josiah reached the Castle of Faith just before nightfall. He reined to a stop at the edge of the moor and sat quietly for a moment as he debated his next move. After thinking it through, he decided not to hide the egg in the hollow tree again. He would take the egg into the castle where it would be safe. Dismounting, he retrieved the egg from his saddle bags and hid it beneath his cloak, holding it against his side in the crook of his elbow. He managed to remount awkwardly.

Turning the mare, he rode across the drawbridge and entered the castle. His heart pounded. He was taking the forbidden egg into King Emmanuel's castle!

A servant met him as he entered the west bailey. "May I take your horse, my lord?"

The young prince turned the mare over to him. "Rub her down well. She's run hard."

Josiah hurried up the stairs toward his solar, determined to hide the egg as quickly as possible. He felt a sense of relief when he reached the room without encountering Selwyn or Gilda. Glancing around quickly, he opened the door and slipped inside. He surveyed the round chamber at a glance. Perhaps he could hide the egg in the fireplace, but then it would get soiled with soot and ashes. The only practical hiding place would be in one of the three drawers of the chiffonnier.

Uneasy at the idea of trying to hide the dragon's egg in his solar, the young prince slipped back out on the sentry walk and closed the door behind him. Glancing furtively around to ascertain that no one was watching, he hurried across the castle grounds, crossed the east bailey, and slipped inside the stables.

The stable boy was attending to the mare as Josiah entered. Moving as quietly as possible, the young prince sneaked across the stable and climbed the ladder to the loft without being seen. He stepped across golden mounds of sweet-smelling hay until he reached the far corner. The perfect hiding place! He dug deeply into the hay, hollowing out a small void in which to hide the egg. He slipped the egg from beneath his cloak.

The dragon's egg began to glow and change color, pulsating and shimmering as he held it. His heart began to pound. Just touching the egg brought a thrill that he couldn't have explained. The egg brought feelings of excitement, adventure, the satisfaction of owning something that perhaps no one else in the kingdom possessed.

At last, he slipped the egg into the hay and carefully buried it, smoothing the hay back into place over the egg and then meticulously dropping bits of hay over the spot to disguise it.

He stepped back, silently surveying the hiding place. The hay looked undisturbed; there was absolutely no sign that anything was secreted there. No one would ever find the dragon's egg. Satisfied that all was well, he managed to slip from the stable without the servant even knowing that he had been there.

He breathed a sigh of relief. The egg was safely hidden inside the castle, and no one had seen him. A nagging doubt haunted the corners of his mind. Possession of a dragon's egg was a direct violation of royal law. He had consciously disobeyed his King, and his conscience troubled him. The egg was hidden, but he still felt uneasy at the thought of keeping it within the castle.

"Josiah." The young prince jumped with fright at the sound of his name. Selwyn hurried across the courtyard. "Gilda and I have been looking for you, Josiah. Where have you been?"

"I—I went out for a ride," Josiah replied, taking a deep breath to quiet the pounding of his heart. He squared his jaw, hoping that his face did not reveal the guilt he felt within.

"You should have invited me," his friend told him. "I would have gone with you."

Josiah just nodded.

In the next few days the young prince began making numerous visits to the hayloft above the stables. Although his conscience bothered him greatly, the egg somehow became irresistible. He had to see it, had to hold it, had to spend time with it. He failed to realize it, but the dragon's egg was slowly taking over his life, slowly seizing control of his heart.

Three weeks after taking the egg into the castle, Josiah again dreamed that Lady Prudence visited his solar. Just as before, she took him through the Lake of Destiny to stand before King Emmanuel. He cringed when the fire revealed the dragon's egg, and he found that he couldn't even look at the face of his King. He awoke in a cold sweat, trembling with emotion.

I'll not keep the dragon's egg a day longer, he resolved. *Tomorrow at first light I shall take it into the forest and crush it once and for all. I must not love that which His Majesty has forbidden.*

He awoke to the song of a meadowlark. Dressing hurriedly, he slipped from his solar and hurried along the sentry walk. He glanced over the castle wall toward the moor. The morning air was cold. A white mist swirled just above the ground and dense clouds of fog obscured the forest and the moor from view.

He hurried to the stable, opening the huge stable door and starting slightly as the hinges squeaked in protest. He wavered just for a moment at the idea of destroying the egg, but then his resolve returned and he quickly climbed the ladder to the loft. He retrieved the egg from its hiding place in the hay. At once it began to glow and pulsate, glowing brighter and brighter until he thought he had never before seen anything so beautiful. *What a shame to destroy such a magnificent egg,* he thought sadly. *Perhaps I shall keep it a while longer.*

At that moment, his thoughts turned to his dream from the night before. He could see King Emmanuel's face, so kind, so loving. He could see the pain that appeared in His Majesty's eyes when the egg emerged from the fire. Once again, he relived his own keen disappointment that he had not heard the words "Well done" from his King.

He set his jaw in determination. "The dragon's egg must be destroyed today," he said aloud, as if attempting to strengthen his own resolve. "I shall not keep it—I shall take it at once to the forest and crush it." The egg glowed brighter and brighter.

He hurried from the stables, crossed the east and west baileys, and entered the castle gatehouse. "Good morning, my lord," a sentry greeted him, reaching for the chain that raised the portcullis. "Out for a morning stroll?"

"Aye," the young prince replied, tight-lipped and not wishing to talk.

Chains rattled as the huge, iron-clad portcullis lifted slowly. Josiah waited impatiently as the sentry unbarred the main gates and swung them slowly open. "Fog's so thick this morning you can hardly see your hand in front of your face," the sentry remarked. "Take care that you do not get lost, my lord."

"I shall not go far," Josiah replied tersely.

He crossed the drawbridge and hurried down the lane toward the moor, his left hand clutching the dragon's egg under the folds of his cloak. His heart cried out at the thought of what he was about to do, but he steeled himself and walked on. He turned. The morning mists had already obscured the Castle of Faith from view.

He stepped into the forest bordering the moor. The sentry was right—the fog was unusually thick. He found that he could barely see two paces in front of him.

He came to a large flat rock two or three yards across. *The perfect place to destroy the egg,* he thought. He knelt and picked up a fist-sized rock with his right hand. Fighting the impulse to take the dragon's egg back into the castle, he pulled the forbidden object from beneath his cloak.

Josiah froze as he heard a cough nearby. The sound came from just a few paces to his left. His heart pounded as he hurriedly thrust the egg back under his cloak. Just then, a young squire materialized out of the mists. "Good morning, my lord," the boy greeted him. "Out for a morning stroll?"

Josiah nodded without speaking.

"Never have I seen a fog such as this," the boy remarked. "One can hardly see one's own hand before his face."

The young prince did not reply. He waited for the squire to move on so that he could finish the task he had set out to do. Instead, the boy seemed inclined to talk. "This is my only time to explore the forest," he told Josiah. "In just a few minutes my knight will be calling me to assist him. I work from morning to night, with nary a moment to call my own. A lad deserves time of his own, wouldn't you say?" The squire rambled on and on, talking about nothing. Josiah, impatient with the boy's idle prattle, replied in monosyllables. He didn't want to be rude, but he was trying not to encourage the strange squire. He desperately wanted the boy to move on so that he could crush the egg.

The young squire rambled on and on with no sign of stopping.

At last, Josiah let the rock fall to the earth. Thoroughly frustrated, he said, "Well, good day, lad. I must be about my business." He turned abruptly and moved away quickly, seeking another place to finish the task of destroying the egg. He paused in a thick grove of trees. *I'll do it here.* He bent over and reached for another rock.

To his dismay, the talkative boy immediately reappeared. "Have you ever seen such a fog, my lord? It's as thick as sweet cream. And the weather is so cool. My knight says that the hens lay better in cool weather."

Josiah groaned. Would the bothersome squire never leave him alone?

Ten minutes later, the young prince was ready to give up. The squire had followed him repeatedly from place to place, never catching the hints Josiah had dropped about wanting to be alone. "Hurry home, lad," he finally told the boy. "Your knight will be waiting for you." He turned abruptly and darted away, hoping that the irksome lad would not be able to follow him through the swirling mists.

He stopped in a thick grove of young evergreens. He stood, listening intently, waiting expectantly, but heard nothing. To his relief, the squire did not make an appearance. He knelt. Taking the dragon's egg from within his cloak, he laid it on the ground. He picked up a large rock. Holding the rock with both hands, he raised it over his head.

At that moment he heard a soft cry, not unlike the mewing of a kitten. He paused, rock poised, listening intently. The plaintive sound came again, a low, mournful cry that stirred an unnamed emotion within his heart. He lowered the rock, turning his head from side to side to determine the origin of the unusual sound.

He stared at the egg. Flashes of color were pulsating weakly across the surface of the egg, slowly growing fainter and fainter as he watched. It was as if the egg was dying. He gulped. Had the strange cries come from the egg?

He picked up the rock, and the soft, mournful cries were repeated. His hands trembled as he dropped the rock harmlessly beside him. For some unknown reason, he no longer had the will to crush the egg. Knowing that possession of the dragon's egg was an offense against King Emmanuel's royal law, he had fully intended to destroy it. But now, after being interrupted and distracted by the young squire, he found that he no longer had the heart to do it.

Standing to his feet, he picked up the egg and once again secreted it beneath his cloak. A sense of failure overwhelmed him as he stepped from the woods and hurried up the lane toward the Castle of Faith. King Emmanuel would have him to destroy the egg—of that he was nearly certain—but he had failed. He had tried, but had somehow not been able to do it.

His head was down and his steps were slow as he climbed the stairs to his solar. Why had he been unable to crush the dragon's egg? Entering his solar, he closed the door behind him and sat on the edge of his bed, defeated and discouraged. He withdrew the dragon's egg from beneath his cloak and placed it on the coverlet beside him.

A knock sounded suddenly at his door, and his heart leaped into his throat. He dropped to his knees beside the bed, seized the egg, and thrust it beneath the bed. Letting out his breath in a long sigh, he stood and turned toward the door. "Come in."

The door opened, and Sir Faithful's bearded face appeared. "Good morning, Prince Josiah. I trust you slept well?"

Josiah nodded. "I slept well, sire."

"May I come in?"

The young prince's heart pounded furiously. "Certainly, sire. Come in."

The castle steward stepped into the solar. "It's a fine day to serve His Majesty, is it not?" He stepped to the window and gazed down at the azure waters of the bay below. After a moment or two, he stepped away from the window and then turned to face Josiah. "Selwyn's worried about you, Josiah, and he asked me to talk with you. He says that you've been withdrawn the last few days, and he's afraid that something's wrong. He says that you've changed somehow—you no longer have the eagerness to serve Emmanuel that he has always known you to have. Would you care to tell me about it?"

Josiah did his best to return the old man's gaze as if he had nothing to hide. "Nothing's wrong, sire. I'm fine."

Josiah dropped his eyes as he said the words, and he struggled to stifle a gasp of astonishment. The dragon's egg had rolled from its hiding place beneath the bed and come to rest against the edge of Sir Faithful's foot. As the young prince watched in alarm, the egg began to glow and pulsate with color. If the elderly steward happened to glance downward, he would immediately see the forbidden dragon's egg!

Chapter Eight

Prince Josiah was near panic. The dragon's egg lay in plain sight upon the floor of the solar, pulsing and glowing so brightly that it seemed that the chamber throbbed with the pulsating colors. He glanced at Sir Faithful, but the old man seemed not to notice that anything was amiss. Josiah fought to avoid looking at the egg. If he could just step close enough to nudge the forbidden egg back under the bed, perhaps it would go undiscovered. He expelled his breath slowly.

"Josiah?" The steward was looking at him closely. "Are you all right, my prince?"

Josiah took a deep breath and tried to calm his racing heart. "I—I'm fine, sire."

"You seem ill at ease."

Josiah forced a smile. "I'm fine, sire, really I am."

He glanced toward the floor and inhaled sharply. The dragon's egg had somehow moved around Sir Faithful's foot and was now rolling slowly, deliberately across the center of the solar floor, almost as if it were trying to be discovered! The young prince glanced at the egg in consternation and then looked away quickly. *How could the egg have possibly gotten around Sir Faithful's foot, unless it had deliberately maneuvered its way there—*

unless it were... alive? He shuddered at the thought.

"Josiah?" Sir Faithful's gentle voice broke through his thoughts. "What's troubling you, my prince? Won't you open your heart to me?"

Josiah simply stared at him without answering. The old man had been his mentor and his dear friend since Josiah's arrival at the Castle of Faith, but the young prince wasn't about to admit that he had disobeyed Emmanuel and obtained a dragon's egg. Sir Faithful studied him for a long moment. Josiah waited uncomfortably.

At last, the steward spoke. "Josiah, you have a visitor. I'm sure you'll be glad to see him." He turned toward the door.

Josiah seized the opportunity at hand. He stooped, grabbed the egg, and thrust it beneath the coverlet of his bed in one quick motion. He was just in time. Sir Faithful opened the door, and Sir Dither stepped into the room.

Josiah was taken aback by the unexpected appearance of the marquis. "Sir Dither!"

"Greetings, my prince," the nobleman said, striding forward to grasp Josiah's hand and shake it warmly. "It's a delight to see you again. My heart has not been the same since your visit to the Castle of Steadfastness, I assure you. My heart is now yielded to His Majesty, and once again I find great delight in his service. I owe you a debt of gratitude, Prince Josiah. His Majesty used your words to draw my heart back to his ways, and I rejoice to be in the service of my King. I came to thank you."

Josiah stood silent, not sure how to respond or what to say. His heart was torn between two emotions—one part of him wanted to rejoice with the marquis, while another part of him felt an overwhelming sense of guilt at the man's words. At that moment, he realized for the first time that his own heart was no longer surrendered to the will of his King. The dragon's egg had drawn his heart away.

Sir Faithful spoke. "I'll leave you two to visit." He turned to Sir Dither. "Won't you join us for breakfast in the great hall?"

The marquis nodded. "Aye, that I will, sire. And I thank you."

"Breakfast should be ready in fifteen minutes or less," the steward told him. "It will bc our pleasure to have you." He left the solar.

The marquis beamed at Josiah. "I owe you a debt of gratitude," he said again. "Please accept a small gift as a token of my appreciation."

"A gift?"

"I'll be honored if you'll accept it." He smiled again. "It's right outside your door."

Josiah followed Sir Dither out onto the sentry walk. To his surprise, a birdcage sat just outside the door. Perched inside the cage was a peregrine falcon. "She's yours, my lord," the marquis said grandly. "But for you, she would have escaped, so it's only right that you should have her."

He stepped close to the cage. "She's quite young, my lord, and not yet fully trained. She comes to the lure quite readily now—" he laughed abruptly— "much better than the day we first met. I'll be here for a few days, and I can show you how to finish training her to hunt."

The young prince moved close to the cage in order to better see the falcon. The bird of prey sat motionless upon her perch, but Josiah could tell that she was watching him closely. He studied the falcon, noting the powerful beak, the stately plumage, and the strong talons. She seemed so elegant, so proud, so powerful. Josiah took a deep breath. "She's beautiful, sire."

Sir Dither smiled. "Owning a falcon is quite a responsibility, my lord. She needs to be flown daily, and she needs to be cared for on a regular basis. In the next few days, I'll tell you more about it and teach you what you need to know about falconry. If you decide that you're willing to undertake the responsibility for her, I'll leave her with you. If not, I'll take her with me when I return to the Castle of Steadfastness."

The falcon stirred slightly, turning her head to look directly at Josiah. "What does she eat, sire?"

"She hunts small game. Grouse, pheasant, partridge and rook, maybe an occasional hare. I've started her on her hunt training, but if I let you take over as trainer, she'll soon hunt readily for you."

The marquis looked at him. "Are you interested in learning falconry?"

Josiah nodded eagerly. "I'd love to."

"Don't be afraid to tell me if you're not interested, my lord. Falconry takes a bit of time and dedication, and some people are just not ready for that much commitment. If you decide that you want the bird, she's yours. If not, tell me before I leave the Castle of Faith and I'll take her back with me.

"Don't try to decide just now; wait until you see what is involved in keeping and caring for a falcon, and then you can let me know."

Two weeks later, Prince Josiah and Sir Dither sat side by side on their horses, eagerly watching the sky. "She's up so high she's hardly more than a dot in the sky," Josiah said breathlessly. "She must be at a pitch of least a thousand feet."

"More than that," the marquis agreed. He pointed a short distance across the moor on which he and Josiah were hunting with the falcon. "Did you see the hare go into that thicket? Let's ride in there and flush him out, and your falcon will get him."

Josiah studied the thicket and then glanced skyward again. "What if she doesn't see it?"

"Oh, she will, my lord," the marquis assured him.

"But she's up so high, sire," the young prince argued. "If she's just a dot to us, the rabbit will be just a tiny dot to her."

"Peregrine falcons have excellent eyesight," the marquis replied. "Watch." He rode forward into the thicket, and a fat hare instantly exploded from the other side, running across the moor as fast as it could go. Josiah lost sight of it as it disappeared behind a small hillock. He rode forward, watching the sky as he did.

The soaring falcon abruptly dropped from the heavens, streaking toward the earth in a breath-taking dive. Within seconds she leveled off above the moor and dropped out of sight behind the rise where the hare had vanished. "Let's go," Sir Dither called, "and see if your falcon made the kill."

Together the marquis and the prince rode across the moor to find the falcon perched on the carcass of the hare. "Another successful binding," Sir Dither said proudly. "Josiah, she's going to make quite a hunter."

"Aye, that she is," the young prince replied, beaming with pleasure. "Sir Dither, this is the first time in my life I have had a pet of my own, and what a grand pet she is! She's magnificent! Did you see how fast she dived from the sky when she saw the hare? One moment she was a thousand feet in the sky, the next moment, she had the hare."

"The peregrine falcon has the fastest stoop of any bird of prey in the kingdom of Terrestria," the marquis replied. "It's always a thrill to watch them hunt."

He dismounted and strode forward to take the dead hare from the falcon. "You two have trained well together," he told the young prince. "I plan to head home tomorrow, and I think you two will get along just fine. Well, shall we feed her and then head back to the castle?"

Half an hour later, back in his solar at the Castle of Faith, Prince Josiah carefully hooded the falcon and placed her back in her cage. "You hunted well today," he proudly told the magnificent bird as he removed the jesses from her legs. "That hare never had a chance. You dropped from the sky like a bolt of lightning and that poor hare was dead before he knew what hit him."

He closed the cage door and then stood studying the falcon. "I think I'll name you 'Lightning', for you're as fast as lightning when you stoop for a kill. Lightning. The name fits you. Lightning, you are one magnificent bird."

Josiah stood studying the falcon for several minutes. His heart swelled with delight at the thought of owning such a magnificent creature. "The sport of kings," he said to Lightning. "That's what Sir Dither calls falconry. And you certainly are a regal bird, worthy of a king. I'm proud to own you."

He walked over and sat on the edge of the bed, idly reaching over to the spot where for the last two weeks he had hidden the dragon's egg beneath his coverlet. The familiar bulge in the coverlet was not there. He moved a pillow, searching for the egg, and noticed that the corner of the coverlet was crumpled and turned back. Mystified, he tossed the pillow to one side and threw back the coverlet.

He gasped in horror. His heart pounded. He trembled uncontrollably as fear washed over him in dark waves. This was worse than his worst nightmare. The unimaginable had happened. Pieces of broken eggshell lay in a small heap beneath the coverlet. In an instant, he realized the awful truth: the dragon's egg had hatched.

Chapter Nine

Prince Josiah stared in dismay at the broken pieces of eggshell. The unthinkable had happened—the dragon's egg had hatched—and the dreadful realization struck him like a blow from a broadsword. The peasant in the forest had assured him that hatching was an impossibility; the egg had been dead for two centuries. But the pieces of broken shell gave evidence that there had indeed been a hatching. He, Prince Josiah, the son of King Emmanuel, was responsible for hatching a Cararian Greatwing dragon. At that very moment, somewhere in the halls and chambers of the Castle of Faith, a young dragon was lurking.

His mind reeled. He was close to panic. How dangerous was a hatchling Cararian Greatwing? Should he alert Sir Watchful, the castle constable, so that the two garrisons of knights could search the castle and destroy the dragon? Should he keep quiet? Were the castle inhabitants in danger?

He took a deep breath and held it, trying to steady himself and calm his pounding heart. If he warned Sir Watchful of the dragon's existence, he would be forced to explain its presence in the castle. The truth would be out, and King Emmanuel would know that he had hatched a dragon. Perhaps it would be better if he could locate the dragon and destroy it himself. Trembling uncontrollably, he drew his sword.

He stepped to the window and peered out. The little dragon could not be more than an hour old, two hours at most. Would a Cararian Greatwing be capable of flying that soon after hatching? Shaking his head, he admitted to himself that he had no way of knowing. He stepped away from the window.

Think, he admonished himself. *This dragon is all your fault! You had better do something, and you had better do it quickly. If the dragon kills or injures someone...* He pushed the thought from his mind. *What should I do? Should I tell Sir Watchful? Should I tell Sir Faithful? The castle residents must be warned, but then, I will have to explain...*

He ran to the solar door, jerked it open, and, standing on the sentry walk, quickly surveyed the west bailey. No dragon. He leaned over the inner wall and hurriedly scanned the barbican between the inner and outer walls. Nothing.

I'll search the castle myself while I determine a course of action, he decided. *If I can find the dragon and destroy it myself, no one else will ever need to know what happened. If I can't find it, well, then I'll have to tell someone.* He hurried down the stairs toward the bailey.

A sentry passed him on the stairs. "Is the castle under attack, my lord?"

Josiah stopped cold. "Under attack?"

"You're rushing down the stairs with a sword in your hand," the knight replied with a hint of a smile. "I thought that perhaps—"

"Oh." Josiah held the weapon against his side. When it transformed itself into the book, he thrust it hastily inside his doublet. Thoroughly embarrassed, he tried to explain. "Nay, we're not under attack, sire. I was just—oh, never mind." He turned and hurried down the stairs.

When he reached the bailey, he glanced back up at the sentry and then hurriedly searched the entire courtyard. No sign of a dragon. He darted to the east bailey and quickly searched, even walking through the shrubbery to make certain that the hatchling dragon was not lurking there. He kept his hand on the book, ready to draw his sword.

He entered the stables. He had kept the egg in the loft—would the dragon have returned there? He darted toward the ladder that led to the loft.

"Prince Josiah, what is your hurry?"

Josiah whirled around, startled at the voice, to find Sir Preparation, the castle armorer, preparing to shoe a horse. The little man laughed. "Don't let me keep you from something important, my prince. You came dashing in here as if you were being pursued by a dragon."

"I—I'm looking for something, sir," Josiah stammered, "and I must admit that I am in a bit of a hurry."

"May I help you find it, my lord?"

Josiah shook his head. "Please continue with your work. I'll find it soon, I'm sure." Hoping that Sir Preparation would be satisfied with the vague explanation, he turned and hurried up the ladder. Struggling to hold back a rising sense of panic, he searched the hayloft as quickly as possible. No dragon. He descended the ladder and searched the stables, moving from stall to stall as rapidly as possible.

"Didn't find it, my lord?" Sir Preparation sympathized. "Please let me know if I may be of assistance."

Josiah nodded. "I thank you, sir." He hurried from the stables.

His mind was in turmoil as he rushed across the bailey to search the great hall. *What shall I do if I cannot find the hatchling?* he worried. *Should I tell Sir Watchful? What will he say when he finds out that I have hatched a dragon? What will Sir Faithful say?*

In twenty desperate minutes the young prince managed to search a large part of the castle. Dashing down corridors, darting up and down stairs, and ducking through doorways, he quickly searched the kitchen, the armory, the garderobes, and even scanned some of the solars, but the young dragon was nowhere to be found. Josiah's anxiety increased as the search progressed. Where could the young dragon have gone?

Perhaps the hatchling has found a way to get out of the castle, he thought. *I need to search the forest and the moors.* He hurried back to the stables.

"Still searching, my lord?" Sir Preparation greeted him. "Perhaps I may help?"

The young prince shook his head. "I just want to take the mare out for a short jaunt."

"Of course, my lord. Allow me to saddle her for you."

Moments later, Josiah reined to a stop at the edge of the castle drawbridge. *Unless the dragon can already fly,* he told himself, *it couldn't have gone far. With the Sea of Conviction to the south and the west of the castle, all I have to do is search the woods and the moors to the north and the east. I doubt if the dragon could have yet reached the village.*

He spent the next thirty minutes riding through the forest and the moors, anxiously scanning the area for any sign of the little dragon. He searched each thicket, each draw, each windbreak, but the creature was not to be found. At last, alarmed at his failure to locate the creature, he returned to the castle. He rode the mare to the stables.

The stable boy took the mare's reins as Josiah dismounted. "I'll rub her down well, my lord," he said, eyeing the horse's sweaty flanks. "You must have ridden her hard."

"Aye, that I did," Josiah replied curtly. He gave the mare a pat on the neck and hurried from the stable.

Back in his solar, he approached the falcon's cage. "I really don't know what to do, Lightning," he said, addressing the bird. "I can't find the dragon anywhere, yet I cannot go to Sir Faithful or Sir Watchful. King Emmanuel must not find out that I have hatched a dragon, for my disobedience would bring sorrow to his heart. I just do not know what to do."

Lightning didn't reply.

The young prince stepped to the window and looked out at the sparkling waters of the bay. "Where can that dragon be?" he asked, thinking aloud. "If the dragon can fly already, it is undoubtedly far away by now. I did not search the entire castle, for some of the solars were occupied, but the dragon could not be there, for it would have been noticed when it entered. I searched the woods and the moors, but perhaps it was able to travel faster and farther than I anticipated." He sighed. "I suppose there is nothing more that I can do."

He turned toward the bed. "I do need to dispose of the eggshells, though." He knelt to retrieve the fragments of eggshell, and at that moment, he thought he heard a faint cry, like the mewing of a kitten. He paused, holding his breath and listening intently. He heard it again. Josiah frowned. This was the same cry he had heard out on the moor when he was about to crush the egg.

He waited, listening intently, but the sound was not repeated. Finally, he shrugged and began gathering the fragments of eggshell from beneath the coverlet. When his hands were full, he realized that he had nowhere to dispose of the pieces without arousing suspicions. *I can't take them to the kitchens or to the trash port,* he told himself, *for someone might see me. The garderobe! I can throw them down the hole in the garderobe.*

Josiah stood and cautiously opened his solar door just a

crack. Putting his eye to the crack, he surveyed the bailey and the sentry walk. *No one is about. If I can just make it over to the garderobe without being seen...*

He froze. The strange cry came again, so faint he could barely hear it and sounding very much like a kitten in distress. The sound was coming from under the bed! Dropping the pieces of eggshell on the coverlet, the young prince knelt and peered beneath the bed. Nothing but shadows.

He frowned. *I heard the sound. I know I did. And it certainly sounded like it was coming from under the bed. But what could be making such a strange noise?* He walked around the other side of the bed, knelt, and peered into the darkness again.

And then he saw it. Huddled against the bed post, almost invisible in the shadows, was a strange little creature unlike anything he had ever seen. The extraordinary creature, whatever it was, had pale, translucent skin, with scaly legs that terminated in claws like a bird. An oversized mouth kept opening and closing. *It looks like a four-legged chicken without feathers or a beak,* the young prince thought. *What a pitiful little thing. I wonder where it came from, and how it got here.*

Trembling and crying softly, the bizarre little creature moved toward the other side of the bed, away from Josiah. *Whatever it is, it's afraid of me,* the young prince realized. *I must move slowly so as not to frighten it.* Dropping to his belly, he crawled slowly under the bed, moving just inches at a time.

Watching Josiah's every move, the little creature crept backwards until it was cornered between the bed and the chiffonnier and could go no further. It sat trembling, watching, bobbing its little head up and down in a pitiful manner. Josiah carefully scooted closer. Spreading his hands wide, he reached toward the little creature, which gave a cry of alarm. Spreading tiny, batlike wings, it tried to scramble away. But the animal was trapped against the wall and could go no further.

Josiah carefully cupped his hands around the trembling creature and gently pulled it toward him. "Don't be frightened, little fellow," he said in a soft, crooning voice. "I won't hurt you."

Drawing the pitiful creature against his chest, Josiah carefully slid from beneath the bed and stood to his feet. He used one hand to create a nest-like opening in the folds of the coverlet and then gently placed the peculiar little animal into it. Immediately the creature ducked its head in an effort to burrow into the material. Josiah cupped his hands around the coverlet, molding the fabric around the trembling body in an attempt to soothe it. He reached out and stroked the little head with one finger.

"Never before have I seen a creature such as you," he said softly. "You're a frail little thing, aren't you? But where did you come from, and how did you ever get into my solar?"

Josiah glanced toward the falcon's cage. "Well, Lightning, it looks as if I now have two pets." He chuckled as he stroked the trembling creature huddled helplessly in the coverlet. "I might have found you sooner, little fellow, but I've been busy searching for a dragon, and—"

He gasped as a sudden realization hit him with the abruptness of an arrow from a longbow. The pitiful creature in his hands was the hatchling dragon. He was holding a baby Cararian Greatwing!

Chapter Ten

Taking the steps two at a time, Prince Josiah hurried toward the great hall for the noon meal. He took a deep breath. The discovery of the hatchling dragon in his solar had been quite a shock, but after the first few moments of anxiety, he had begun to relax. The dragon was, after all, quite a helpless, pitiful creature, hardly a threat to anyone in the Castle of Faith. There was no cause for alarm.

The little dragon had settled down quite comfortably in the nest that Josiah had created with his bed sheets and coverlet. Hidden beneath the bedclothes, the dragon was not readily visible from the solar door, should anyone open it unexpectedly, and the eggshell had been disposed of by throwing the pieces down the hole in the garderobe. Josiah felt that his secret was quite safe.

"Josiah, wait for us," a voice called, and the young prince turned to see Prince Selwyn and Princess Gilda hurrying to catch up with him. "What have you been doing all morning?" Selwyn asked. "We haven't seen you around the castle."

Josiah shrugged. "I hunted the falcon for awhile," he answered evasively. "By the way, I decided to name her 'Lightning'."

"Lightning," Gilda repeated. "That's a strange name for a bird."

"When you see her hunt you'll understand," Josiah replied. "One minute she'll be soaring high in the heavens, but when she spots quarry, she strikes like lightning. It's incredible."

"She's an amazing bird, isn't she?" Selwyn observed.

Josiah nodded. "It's a thrill to own her."

"When is Sir Dither going back to the Castle of Steadfastness?" Gilda asked.

"He left this morning," Josiah replied. He turned to Selwyn. "What do dragons eat?"

"Dragons?" Selwyn's face registered his surprise. "What makes you ask that?"

Josiah shrugged. "I don't know. I guess it's just something I've always wondered."

Selwyn laughed. "I have no idea, Josiah. I don't suppose it matters, as long as one doesn't decide to eat me."

Gilda shuddered.

Josiah held the door of the great hall for Gilda and Selwyn.

"Sir Faithful would undoubtedly know what dragons eat," Selwyn suggested, as the three friends strolled across the massive hall toward the King's table.

Josiah quickly shook his head. "It doesn't matter."

The castle residents took their places around the tables and Sir Faithful sent a petition of thanksgiving to King Emmanuel. A procession of attendants filed in bearing platters of roast mutton, pheasant in cinnamon sauce, beef fritters, filets of saltwater fish, and various garden vegetables. Josiah took some of each, nearly filling his trencher. Selwyn and Gilda's trenchers were just as full. An attendant approached with a huge silver platter, on which were various sauces and fruit jellies.

As they started eating, Selwyn turned to Sir Faithful, who was seated at the end of the table. "Sire, what do dragons eat?"

All conversation at the table stopped abruptly. The lords and ladies looked at Selwyn in bewilderment.

Josiah inhaled sharply. *Don't ask that question,* he pleaded silently.

Sir Faithful gave Selwyn a strange look. "What do dragons eat? Whatever makes you ask a question like that, lad?"

Selwyn shrugged. "Josiah and I were just wondering."

The steward took a long drink from his goblet. "Dragons often eat sheep, cattle, harts, maybe an occasional dog or cat. They've even been known to eat humans."

Gilda gasped.

"What would a baby dragon eat?" The question popped out before Josiah could stop it.

Sir Faithful frowned. "Why the sudden interest in dragons?"

The young prince shrugged without answering.

"Young dragons would eat smaller animals, of course. Mice, rats, squirrels, that sort of thing. As a dragon increases in size, his appetite increases, of course, and he eats larger and larger prey. An adult dragon could even eat a horse."

Gilda shuddered. "Can we talk about something else?"

The steward smiled. "Of course, my lady. I'm not sure why this even came up for discussion." He gave Selwyn and Josiah a stern look.

That afternoon Josiah lay silently in the hayloft, ear pressed against the hay, listening intently. The stirring, scratching sound came again, followed by tiny squeaks, so faint he could barely hear them. He rose to his knees and dug quickly into the hay. Suddenly, a mouse darted from beneath his hands and scampered to safety. Josiah grinned as he lifted the last clump of hay, exposing the mouse's nest. Five little pink mice lay in the nest, blind and hairless. Josiah scooped them up.

Two minutes later, back in his solar, he carefully pulled back the coverlet, exposing the baby dragon. The little creature cowered away from him and tried to bury itself in the sheets. "It's all right, little fellow," Josiah crooned softly. "Look what I brought you."

Opening his cupped hands, he grasped a pinkie mouse with the thumb and forefinger of his right hand, clutching the other four mice carefully in his left. He held the pinkie out toward the little dragon. "Are you hungry, little fellow? I brought you something to eat."

Josiah jumped as the little dragon snapped the pinkie mouse from his hands, swallowing it in two gulps. He quickly pulled out another and offered that to the hatchling. "You were hungry, weren't you?"

In no time at all the five mice were gone. "I see that you have teeth," Josiah said to the dragon. "Perhaps you're not as helpless as you look." The hatchling nuzzled against his hand as if seeking more food. "That's all I brought," the young prince told the creature apologetically. "I didn't even know if you were ready to eat. I'll get you some more later."

In the next few weeks, Josiah spent much of his time hunting food for the dragon. The little beast progressed from eating pinkie mice to full-grown mice and rats and then to squirrels and young rabbits. The young prince was hard pressed to keep up with the creature's demands for food. He still took the time to take the falcon hunting daily, as her kills provided some of the necessary food for the dragon.

The young prince was alarmed at how quickly the dragon had grown. "You must weigh at least two stone now," he told the young dragon one day, watching as it greedily devoured a pheasant. "I don't know how much longer I can keep you."

The dragon arched its back, spread its wings wide, and hissed angrily. Josiah took a step backwards. The creature's wings, hardly as big as a baby's hands when it was first hatched, were now nearly six feet across. *No wonder it is called a Cararian Greatwing,* he thought. *His wings are bigger than his body. I wonder how much larger they will get.*

He studied the dragon. The pale, translucent skin of the young hatchling had been replaced by a tough, leathery hide, greenish gray in color. Josiah could see that scales were beginning to form over most of the body and that the tail was beginning to lengthen. The tiny teeth of the infant had been replaced with teeth nearly an inch long. *This creature will be quite ferocious when it is full-grown,* he thought. *I must not allow it to reach maturity.*

The dragon continued hissing. "Stop it at once," Josiah ordered sternly, moving toward the beast. "I am the one who feeds you. Don't you hiss at me." The dragon lowered its head and went back to eating the pheasant, stopping from time to time to look sulkily at Josiah.

There came a sudden knock at the door, and Josiah's heart seemed to stop. Snatching the pheasant carcass from the dragon, he thrust it under the bed. The dragon crouched and squeezed under the bed after it. "Stay under there," Josiah ordered. "Don't come out for anything." He opened the door to find Selwyn standing there.

"You said we could take Lightning out for a hunt today," Selwyn said, brushing past Josiah and striding into the room. "Are you still planning on it?"

"Aye," Josiah replied, trying to think of a way to get his friend out of the solar as quickly as possible. The dragon was under the bed, noisily devouring what remained of the pheasant. If Selwyn should hear it...

"What's that noise?" Selwyn asked, with a puzzled look on his face.

"I have to get Lightning ready," Josiah said quickly. "Would you mind waiting outside? She's not accustomed to having anyone other than me here and you might make her a bit anxious. She won't hunt well if she's not relaxed. Do you mind?"

Selwyn shrugged. "I'll wait for you in the bailey." He slipped outside.

Josiah gave a sigh of relief as the door closed behind him. "That was close!" His hands were shaking as he opened the cage and attached the jesses to the falcon's legs. He hooded the falcon, put on his handling glove, and called to the bird. Lightning stepped from her perch to Josiah's arm. Josiah picked up the lure and the creance. "Ready to hunt, girl? It's time. I want you to put on a good show for Selwyn."

Ten minutes later, the two young princes rode slowly across the moors. High above them, Lightning soared across the heavens. Selwyn gazed upward at the majestic falcon. "She's awfully high, Josiah. If we flush any game, how will she see it?"

Josiah laughed. "Lightning can see a sparrow from that height," he said proudly. "She could even spot a mouse from there."

Selwyn stared at his companion in astonishment. "Are you certain?"

"Peregrine falcons have incredible eyesight. I've seen Lightning spot small game when she was much higher than that."

Selwyn gave a low whistle to express his astonishment. "That's incredible!"

"She's a magnificent bird, Selwyn. Sometimes I have a hard time believing that she's actually mine. When I hunt her, I experience feelings that... well, I feel like a king or something. And I think she enjoys hunting for me, or at least, I want to think that she does. We've become quite a team, Lightning and I."

"Perhaps someday I will have a falcon of my own," Selwyn said wistfully.

"I'll help you train it if you do," Josiah promised.

Just then a partridge exploded from the thicket in front of them, flying low and fast as it sought another place of refuge. Josiah stood in the stirrups. "Watch."

The soaring falcon abruptly dropped from the heavens, streaking toward the earth in a breath-taking dive. Seconds later she struck the fleeing partridge in an explosion of flying feathers. Josiah rode forward, dismounted, and took the dead bird from the falcon. "Good girl, Lightning. You hunted well."

Selwyn joined him. "That was incredible, Josiah! The partridge didn't stand a chance. Lightning struck it like a... well, like a bolt of lightning out of the sky!"

Josiah grinned. "She's incredible, isn't she?"

Selwyn glanced at the game bird in Josiah's hand. "Why didn't you let her eat the partridge?"

"We hunt falcons when they're hungry," Josiah replied. "I'll feed her when we get back to the castle. I'll send her up again for another hunt in just a few minutes."

"What are you going to do with the partridge?"

"I'll take it back to the castle," Josiah replied, not wishing to tell Selwyn that it was food for the dragon. "Someone can use it, I'm sure."

Five minutes later the boys flushed a rabbit. Just as before, the falcon swooped down and quickly killed it. Josiah placed the rabbit in the game bag with the pheasant. He mounted the mare and called Lightning to him. Immediately the falcon flew up and perched on his arm. "Let's find some more game," he told Selwyn. "I'll show you how well she bates."

"Bates?"

"Bating is when she hunts from a perch or from my arm," Josiah explained. "It's almost as exciting as when she stoops from high altitude."

Just then, the clear call of a trumpet sounded across the moor. Selwyn glanced up toward the Castle of Faith. "The call to arms! It came from the castle. Let's go!"

The hunt was forgotten as the two young princes wheeled their mounts and galloped at full speed across the moor. The horses' hooves beat a staccato rhythm on the drawbridge as they rode swiftly into the castle. They reined to a stop in the west bailey, which was quickly filling with spirited horses. The two garrisons of knights were preparing to ride into battle.

Lord Watchful met Selwyn and Josiah. "Argamor's forces are attacking the Castle of Virtue," he told them. "We ride in ten minutes."

Josiah dismounted and dropped the reins. Leaving the mare standing, he dashed for his solar with Lightning perched on his left shoulder and the game bag in his right hand. He took the stairs two at a time. Entering the solar, he dropped the game bag on the floor and hurriedly returned the falcon to her cage. "I'll have to feed you later," he apologized as he removed her jesses. He dumped the pheasant and the rabbit on the floor and thrust them under the bed for the dragon. He was breathing hard as he swiftly donned the various pieces of his armor.

Ten minutes later, two columns of knights astride powerful white chargers rode swiftly from the Castle of Faith, their armor gleaming brightly in the afternoon sun. King Emmanuel's royal purple banner with the emblem of the cross and crown flew grandly from Lord Watchful's lance. The Castle of Faith was riding to the assistance of the Castle of Virtue.

"Argamor told his warriors at the council of war that they would not be attacking Emmanuel's castles directly," Josiah remarked to Selwyn, who rode to his left. "He and the Council of Six had decided that it was more effective to attempt to wrest the kingdom from King Emmanuel by targeting individual subjects and stealing their hearts away. Why is he attacking the Castle of Virtue?"

"The Castle of Virtue is in a strategic location, just as is the Castle of Faith," another knight replied, overhearing Josiah's question. "Argamor is still concentrating on stealing the hearts of the men of the kingdom, but he is also making direct assaults on certain of the castles. He's waging war on two fronts, as it were. As knights to His Majesty, we have the responsibility to not only protect the castles, but also to guard our own hearts."

After a hard ride of nearly half an hour, the cavalcade of knights rode over the crest of a rocky hill. Lord Watchful reined to a stop, and the two columns of knights fell in behind him. In the valley before them sprawled a sleepy village. On the opposite side of the valley, the Castle of Virtue, a concentric stone castle very similar in appearance to the Castle of Faith, perched high above the town on a precipitous mountainside. The approach to the gatehouse was extremely steep and difficult. From their vantage, Lord Watchful and his knights could see that the castle was under attack by bands of knights in dark armor.

"We fight for the sake of our brethren," Lord Watchful called, "and for the honor and glory of King Emmanuel. Stand valiant in battle, men, and trust in the power of your King. Let's ride!"

The garrisons of knights rode forward, galloping at full speed through the village and then urging their powerful warhorses up the steep slope on the opposite side. Prince Josiah felt a surge of excitement. He was riding into battle for King Emmanuel! Reaching within his breastplate, he withdrew the book and swung it vigorously. In an instant, the book was transformed into a glittering sword.

A band of dark knights was attacking the gates of the Castle of Virtue with a battering ram. Holding the stout battering ram at shoulder height, they charged forward, slamming the end of the ram into the massive gates with a crash that resounded across the hillside. The gates shook with the impact. Moving in unison, the dark knights carried the ram backward several paces and then charged forward with all their might, again smashing the battering ram ferociously into the gates.

Several more dark knights had placed scaling ladders against the walls at several points and were attempting to scale the walls. Archers atop the castle walls were releasing a constant barrage of arrows as they struggled to defend the castle. A smaller group of knights was pouring boiling water from atop the wall as they endeavored to stop the assault on the main gate.

A huge catapult had been placed in position in the valley at a point some hundred yards from the castle. As Lord Watchful and the King's knights rode furiously across the valley, the long arm of the catapult abruptly swung skyward, releasing a huge boulder into the air. Josiah watched as the projectile soared over the walls to land within the Castle of Virtue with a crash that resounded across the valley. He winced.

Lord Watchful called a halt and the knights sat tall in the saddle as they waited for instructions. "Captain Diligence and his garrison will follow me to the main gate," the constable ordered, "as we take that battering ram out of commission. Captain Assurance, your garrison is to capture and destroy that catapult. Gentlemen, fight for the glory of your King! We prevail only in the power of his name."

Josiah and Selwyn rode with the garrison assigned to the catapult. Hooves pounding, they swept across the valley toward the dark knights manning the massive weapon of war. The dark knights drew swords as the King's men approached, but Josiah felt no fear. In his hand he held the invincible sword given him by the Lord of Terrestria.

After a moment's fierce conflict several dark knights lay dead or wounded upon the ground. Josiah felt a surge of elation. The battle was theirs; the dark knights were falling back before them!

He heard a battle cry from behind and turned his horse. His heart pounded with fear. Sweeping across the valley floor directly toward them was a huge cavalcade of mounted knights in dark armor! Within seconds, he and his companions were surrounded by fierce hordes of the enemy armed with swords and battle axes.

A horseman rode at full gallop straight toward Josiah. The young prince swung his sword with all his might. To his dismay, the mighty blow glanced harmlessly off the man's helmet. The enemy knight swung his sword. Josiah raised his Shield of Faith just in time.

Josiah swung again, but the results were the same. The other knight easily repelled the blow and then returned a blow of his own that caught the young prince in the side, piercing his armor and wounding him. Josiah looked around for help but could see none of his companions from the Castle of Faith. In panic, he turned his horse.

A mighty blow across the neck knocked him from the saddle.

He landed flat on his back with a bone-jarring impact and the crash of armor. His sword clattered to the ground beside him. Desperately, he rolled to his knees, searching for the weapon. The dark knight rode down upon him, sword drawn, intending to take off his head.

At that moment, another dark knight crashed at full gallop into Josiah's adversary, sending both knights tumbling. Josiah seized his sword and scrambled under a nearby thicket. Wounded, dazed, and terrified, the young prince lay face down upon the ground, trying to catch his breath and gather his strength. Blood flowed from his wounds. He managed to rise to his knees. A wave of dizziness engulfed him, and the battlefield before him seemed to spin crazily. The sword fell from his hand.

His mind began to clear and he slowly became aware of the fact that the two dark knights were searching for him. Panic seized him. He was wounded, perhaps seriously, and he knew that he was in no condition to fight. He had dropped his sword. If the enemy knights found him he would not survive this battle.

A petition! He must send a petition to King Emmanuel! Fighting the pain and dizziness, he rose to his knees and crept through the undergrowth, desperately seeking his sword. He could hear the enemy knights coming closer and closer to his hiding place. At last, his groping fingers found the sword, and he grasped it eagerly.

He drew the weapon close. In an instant it transformed itself into the book. Hastily he opened the book and withdrew the parchment. Lacking the time and ability to write a message, he simply rolled the parchment tightly. His Majesty would receive the wordless petition and recognize it as a cry for help. The petition was his only hope.

Josiah opened his trembling fingers and released the petition. To his great dismay, the parchment fell from his hand to land in the dirt. Horrified, the young prince stared at the futile petition, knowing in his heart that King Emmanuel had not received his cry for help.

With the sounds of battle ringing in his ears, Josiah struggled to his feet. The battlefield seemed to spin in a green blur around him. He shook his head in a feeble attempt to clear his mind. *You have to get out of here,* he told himself. *The dark knights will be here in just a minute! You can't let them find you here or you're a dead man!* A misty darkness was threatening to overcome him, rendering him unconscious, but he fought against it. He fell to his knees.

Dizzy and disoriented, Josiah again struggled to his feet and stumbled forward twenty or thirty yards. His trembling legs gave out almost immediately and he sank to the ground. *Go on, go on,* he willed his body. *You have to get out of here! You have to find Lord Watchful and the rest of the garrison. Keep moving, Josiah! You can do it!*

The swirling darkness overcame him and he fell headlong to the ground.

Chapter Eleven

Prince Josiah slowly became aware of a gentle hand caressing his burning brow. The touch was cool and comforting. He opened his eyes. He was on his back, staring up into the worried face of Selwyn. His friend was gently wiping his face with a cool, wet cloth. "What happened?" Josiah whispered feebly.

"Argamor's men nearly killed you," a gruff voice said, and the young prince turned to see Lord Watchful leaning over him. "If Selwyn hadn't reached you in time, you would have been a casualty in the battle."

The battle! It all came back in a flash. He had been engaged in a battle for the Castle of Virtue. "Did—did we lose the battle?" he asked fearfully. "Did Argamor's forces take the Castle of Virtue?"

"The castle is safe," the constable assured him. "The victory was Emmanuel's."

Josiah gave a sigh of relief.

"We were hopelessly outnumbered, but the enemy could not stand before us. As His Majesty promised us in the book, there is no restraint to Emmanuel to save by many or by few. Argamor's forces were defeated."

"What went wrong, Josiah?" Selwyn asked him. "You fought

fiercely, yet you seemed to have no strength in the battle. Why were the dark knights able to overcome you so easily?"

"If you saw that I was in trouble, why did you not come to my aid sooner?" Josiah demanded.

"I came as fast as I could," his friend replied, "though I had to fight my way through an entire regiment of dark knights to reach you."

"You owe your life to Selwyn," Lord Watchful said quietly.

"Selwyn, I thank you," Josiah told his friend. He reached with one hand and touched his wounded side, finding to his amazement that the wound had been bandaged. "How—how did this bandage get here?" he asked in bewilderment.

"You have been unconscious for quite some time," Lord Watchful replied. "We moved you into the Castle of Virtue to attend to your wounds." Josiah looked around and saw to his surprise that he was in an unfamiliar solar.

"Can you tell me why you could not stand against Argamor's men?" Lord Watchful asked, leaning quite close and studying Josiah's face. "You had the sword of Emmanuel, yet you fell before a band of the dark knights. Tell me, my prince, why were you not victorious in battle?"

Josiah felt as if the constable's eyes were burning into his soul. He dropped his gaze. "I—I do not know, sire."

"Prince Josiah, is your heart yielded to the will of His Majesty? His strength is your strength when your heart is yielded."

Josiah didn't answer. He thought of the Cararian Greatwing dragon hidden in his solar. Suddenly he knew that his disobedience had cost him the victory in the battle for the Castle of Virtue.

"Rest awhile," the stalwart knight told him gently. "We will return to the Castle of Faith tomorrow at first light."

Josiah's wounds were not life-threatening. The physician at the Castle of Virtue provided an application of the Balm of Gilead, and to Josiah's surprise, the wounds had healed by the time the garrisons reached the Castle of Faith. As Lord Watchful pointed out, though, he now had scars that would last a lifetime.

It was mid-morning as Lord Watchful and the knights crossed the drawbridge and rode into the castle bailey. Servants met the weary warriors and took their horses. Josiah swung down from the saddle and approached Selwyn as he stood beside his horse. "Thank you, my dear friend," he said sincerely. "You saved my life, and I am grateful."

"You once saved mine," Selwyn responded. "Josiah, I am thankful for your friendship. Apparently, we need each other more than either of us realize."

Josiah laughed. "Certainly I needed you yesterday on the battlefield. I am thankful that you rode to my aid. Selwyn, I am grateful for what you did for me." He thumped Selwyn on the shoulder with a gauntleted fist and then turned away.

The young prince walked slowly across the bailey toward his solar. *I must be rid of the dragon once and for all,* he determined. *Yesterday I had no strength on the battlefield because of that wretched creature. What if Selwyn had not ridden to my aid? What if my disobedience had caused us to lose the Castle of Virtue to Argamor's forces?*

He climbed the stairs slowly. *Owning the dragon gives me a mysterious thrill that I cannot explain. I must admit that I rather enjoy having the beast, even though I know that King Emmanuel has forbidden it. But is it worth it? My sword was not effective on the battlefield. I failed my King. I nearly lost my life. How can I cling to that which can cost me so dearly?*

He paused with his hand upon the latch. *I will destroy the dragon once and for all,* he decided. *I will take the wretched beast into the forest and destroy it with my own sword. Then I will be effective once again for my King.*

He opened the door. To his chagrin, the dragon was perched upon his chiffonnier. The young prince was almost certain that the dragon was noticeably larger than he had been the previous day. "Stay under the bed," Josiah ordered. "If someone should open the door and see you..." The creature hopped down upon the bed and then down to the floor.

Josiah approached the falcon's cage. "Lightning, I'm sorry I neglected to feed you yesterday. We had to ride to the defense of another castle, and there just wasn't time." He picked up the jesses and opened the cage door. "Let's go hunting. I'll feed you immediately afterward, I promise."

Ten minutes later the falcon was soaring majestically across the heavens. Prince Josiah rode across the moors in an attempt to flush game, but his heart was not really in the hunt. He was thinking about the battle of the day before. *What if we had lost the Castle of Virtue to Argamor because of me? I was almost killed because I was weak in battle, and I'm certain that is due to having the dragon in my solar. Once we have completed this hunt and I have fed Lightning, I must take the dragon into the forest and destroy it.*

A large hare darted from the bushes at the edge of the moor and bounded away, seeking another place of concealment. In an instant, the falcon was upon it. Josiah took the carcass from the falcon and then rewarded the bird with a tidbit of meat that the castle cook had given him. "Let's go home, Lightning. This is enough hunting for one day."

Slinging the hare over the back of the saddle and calling the falcon to him, Josiah rode toward home. He dreaded what he had to do. There was something satisfying, something thrilling about owning a Cararian Greatwing, and yet, he had already seen some of the consequences of keeping the dragon. His mind was made up—he would destroy the creature this very day—but his heart cried out at the thought.

After tethering the mare in the west bailey, Josiah carried the falcon and the hare up the stairs to his solar. He met a sentry coming down. "How was the hunting today, my lord?"

"Fair," the young prince replied. "She took one hare. We didn't stay out long."

"She's a magnificent bird, my lord."

The sentry passed on, and Josiah hurried toward his solar. As he entered the chamber he slung the hare under the bed for the dragon. He placed food in Lightning's cage and allowed her to eat while he removed the jesses. When she had finished eating he replaced her hood and secured the cage door. "You're a fine bird, Lightning. You're magnificent when you hunt."

Josiah shook open a large game bag that Sir Dither had given him. If he did it just right, perhaps the dragon would fit inside the bag for the trip to the forest. Hearing a slight noise, he turned. The dragon was perched atop the chiffonnier again, wings spread wide. Josiah groaned. The creature now had a wingspan of at least seven feet. *I had not realized that it had grown so rapidly,* he thought. *It may not fit into the sack, after all. And it may not like the idea of being stuffed inside a broadcloth sack.*

"I want you to take me to the forest," the dragon said, slowly fanning its great wings as it spoke. "I need to learn to fly, and I need to learn to hunt."

"Why must you go to the forest to learn to fly?" Josiah asked.

"This solar is much too small for a great dragon such as I," the creature replied, hopping into the window and looking down upon the sea below. "And if I try my first flight from this window, I might fall into the sea and perish."

"I was planning to take you—" Josiah stopped in midsentence and stared at the dragon. "You spoke! You spoke to me, did you not?"

"Of course I spoke," the dragon replied impatiently. "Why do you find that so amazing?" The voice was that of an indignant child.

"But—" Josiah was at a loss for words. "But you never said anything before. I did not know that you could speak."

"I have been learning your language—your spoken language, and the language of your heart." The creature folded its wings. "Now, are we going to the forest?"

"I was planning to take you there," the young prince told the creature. "Do you think you can fit into this sack?"

The dragon gave an indignant squawk. "Do you perceive me as a mere animal, your pet, perhaps? You may carry me upon your shoulder, as you did this common bird."

"I cannot do that," Josiah protested. "The residents of the castle must not see you. They must not know of your existence."

The dragon exhaled sharply as if offended by Josiah's words. "I see. Very well; you may place me within the sack this once."

Josiah spread the sack open, and the dragon stepped into it, folding its wings tightly around its body. Josiah drew the sack over the dragon's head and pulled the drawstring closed. "You barely fit," he told the creature. "Do not move. I will let you out once we reach the forest."

He hefted the sack over his shoulder, staggering a bit under the weight. "You must weigh more than five stone now. I have been feeding you far too well." He hurried from the solar, down the castle stairs, and across the bailey to the spot where the mare waited patiently. As he set the sack upon the ground, the horse suddenly shied away, side-stepping as if afraid of the sack.

Gripping the sack with both hands, the young prince lifted it high to throw it across his saddle. The mare shied away so violently that he missed the saddle completely and nearly dropped the sack. "Stand still," he ordered the mare. "There's nothing to be afraid of." The mare backed away until she was against the castle wall and could go no further.

Josiah finally managed to lift the sack across the saddle. The mare was agitated and began stepping about nervously. Her ears twitched. She tossed her head. Josiah moved the sack forward and swung into the saddle. "Calm down," he said irritably. "The sack will be empty when we come back."

As Josiah rode through the castle gate, the sentry eyed the sack curiously but said nothing about it. "Have a pleasant ride, my lord." Josiah nodded to acknowledge the greeting and rode on.

Determined to do the deed well out of sight of the castle, Josiah rode north across the moor and then entered the forest to the east. After riding a furlong or two into the forest, he came to an outcropping of rock in a large clearing. He dismounted and lowered the sack to the ground. Drawing his sword, he placed it on a nearby stump. He took a deep breath as he opened the sack.

The dragon emerged from the sack, stretching its neck and unfurling its wings. "A truly ignoble mode of traveling for a Cararian Greatwing such as I," it said, stretching to its full height as it took in its surroundings. Josiah stepped toward the stump and reached for the sword.

Spotting the outcropping of rock, the dragon darted across

to it and scrambled to the top. Perched some eight or nine feet above the ground, it spread its great wings and then slowly raised and lowered them several times as if trying them out. Leaning forward, the dragon jumped from the ledge and glided to the ground fifteen or twenty yards away. Immediately it dashed back to the rock and climbed to the top. Spreading its great wings once more, the creature began to flap them rapidly up and down. With a cry of delight, the dragon lifted into the air, hovered for a moment, and then flew a short distance before alighting on the ground.

"This appears to be a skill easily learned," the dragon said, as it passed Josiah on its way to the rock. "If birds do it, dragons should excel at it."

Within minutes, the dragon was soaring above the treetops. Josiah held his sword against his side, and then replaced it within his doublet as it became a book. The opportunity to slay the dragon had passed; somehow he had not been able to bring himself to do the deed.

He gazed skyward. Several hundred feet in the air, the dragon was rapidly growing smaller and smaller as it flew due north. Moments later, it was completely out of sight. Josiah's heart leaped. Here was his opportunity to escape the wretched creature once and for all! The dragon had never seen the outside of the Castle of Faith—it had entered as an egg and exited inside the game sack—so it would have no way of recognizing the structure as the home of the young prince. If he could reach the castle before the dragon returned, he could successfully abandon it.

Leaping into the saddle, Josiah raced for home. As he crossed the drawbridge, he glanced over his shoulder. The sky was empty; he had outwitted the dragon and lost it forever. He reined to a canter as he entered the gatehouse.

The sentry ran forward. "Are you being pursued, my lord? Shall I secure the gate and sound the call to arms?"

Josiah laughed as he reined the mare to a stop. "Nay, there is no cause for alarm, sir. I was simply running the mare. Everything is fine. Just fine."

A servant approached and the young prince turned the mare over to him. His heart was light as he took the stairs two at a time. He was free of the dragon. In his heart he knew that he would miss the creature, but at the same time, there was a tremendous sense of relief. He had managed to dispose of a Cararian Greatwing without Selwyn or anyone else in the Castle of Faith being the wiser.

He opened the solar door. "Well, Lightning," he said expansively, "I guess there's more than one way to dispose of a Cararian Greatwing."

Raucous laughter greeted his statement, and he turned. To his horror, the young dragon sat perched in the window, slowly folding and unfolding its wings. The creature fixed its gaze upon the young prince and Josiah was certain that he saw derision in its eyes. "You underestimate me, Prince Josiah."

Chapter Twelve

Prince Selwyn, Princess Gilda, and Prince Josiah rode swiftly across the moor in an attempt to keep pace with the falcon. High overhead, Lightning majestically rode the air currents on motionless wings. Josiah glanced skyward, and a thrill of pride surged through his being at the sight of the swift bird of prey.

"There." Gilda reined in and pointed to a shallow, brush-choked ravine along the edge of a meadow. "Doesn't that look like a good hiding place for quarry?"

Josiah nodded as he reined in beside her. "Let's try it. Spread out, and we'll ride through it about ten yards apart."

The girl glanced skyward. "Isn't Lightning flying awfully high to be hunting? If we chase any animals out, how will she see them from up there?"

Her brother laughed. "That's the same thing I thought the first time Josiah took me falconing. Peregrine falcons have excellent eyesight, and can spot prey from great altitudes. If we flush anything, she won't miss it."

Josiah glanced upward and barely managed to stifle a gasp. Some distance to the west, a large, dark silhouette glided silently across the sky and disappeared above the treetops. The dragon was flying across the moors!

"Josiah!" Selwyn grabbed his arm. "I thought I saw a dragon!" He pointed.

Josiah's heart was pounding madly, but he struggled to keep his face from betraying him. He laughed casually. "A dragon? Selwyn, you can't be serious! There are no dragons in these parts."

Selwyn's face showed his bewilderment as he studied the sky. "I only saw a glimpse, but it certainly looked like a dragon to me. Gilda, did you see it?"

Gilda shook her head. "It must have been a sparrow," she teased. "If one has a good imagination, they often look like dragons."

"I'm serious," the young prince insisted. "I think I saw a dragon. It just went soaring over the trees there to the west, just beyond the Village of Dedication."

Josiah laughed again. "Perhaps I should send Lightning after it. She's experienced at killing dragons."

Selwyn frowned with displeasure, but said nothing. Glancing skyward once more, he rode forward. Josiah gave a quiet sigh of relief as he followed his friend.

Two pheasants exploded from the thickets as the three young riders entered the ravine. Moments later, the falcon had brought one to the earth. Gilda shuddered. "It—it happens so suddenly. She strikes like a bolt of lightning, doesn't she?"

Josiah dismounted and took the pheasant from the falcon. "Good girl, Lightning. Ready to hunt again? We'll see what else we can flush for you." The falcon took to the skies again as the young prince remounted and thrust the kill into his game bag.

Within half an hour, the falcon had taken a grouse, a duck, and a hare. The three young riders had flushed another pheasant, but it had somehow managed to get away. Josiah hefted the game bag. "Well, that's probably enough for one day. Let's head back to the castle and feed Lightning." He hooded the falcon and then allowed it to perch on his shoulder.

Selwyn stood in the stirrups, gazing intently to the west. "I want to look for that dragon. It will take only a few minutes."

Josiah laughed scornfully. "Are you still thinking that you actually saw a dragon? Gilda's right, Selwyn—it was probably just a bird or something."

His friend looked pained. "Please don't mock me, Josiah. I'm not sure what I saw, but I'm sure it wasn't a bird. What will it hurt if we ride over and search the forest for a moment? It's hardly three furlongs from here."

Josiah shrugged. The last thing he needed was for Selwyn to find the dragon, but he couldn't refuse without arousing Selwyn's suspicions. "All right. If it will make you happy, we'll search. But just for a minute or two."

The young prince had to admit that he was a bit anxious as he, Gilda, and Selwyn rode through the Village of Dedication and entered the forest to the west. What if they did find the dragon? Suppose it called out to him? What would his friends think of him once they learned that he had actually hatched a Cararian Greatwing?

The three riders entered the forest. Selwyn began searching the forest in earnest, while Gilda and Josiah simply rode along behind and waited for him.

"That bush over there looks rather like a dragon, don't you think, Selwyn?" Josiah called. "Perhaps that was what you saw—a flying bush."

Selwyn didn't answer.

After a few moments, Gilda called, "Selwyn, let's go home. You're never going to find your dragon this way."

Her brother turned his horse. "You're right. We might as well go back."

Josiah rode alongside Selwyn. "I'm sorry if we made fun of you just a bit," he said. "But this dragon thing just seems a bit... well, your imagination is getting the best of you."

"You fought the dragon Authades a few months ago," Selwyn replied evenly. "Did Authades merely exist in your imagination?"

"Authades was more than just a mere shadow," Josiah retorted. "That's all you saw today—just a shadow."

"Perhaps we ought to tell Sir Faithful that you saw a dragon," Gilda suggested.

"Nay!" Josiah blurted. Gilda and Selwyn looked at him strangely. "That is, I—I mean, Sir Faithful is a very busy man. We shouldn't trouble him with this until we know that there really is a dragon."

His friend shrugged. "It looked like a dragon to me. I think we ought to tell him."

Josiah snorted. "If we run to Sir Faithful every time we think we see something out of the ordinary, he's going to think we're a bunch of foolish children! I still say we should wait. If there really is a dragon in this region, others in the castle will spot it. If there isn't, you'll make the three of us look like fools."

Selwyn sighed. "All right. I won't say anything." He grinned suddenly. "But I still say that it was a dragon!"

Josiah laughed.

"Let's head home," Gilda suggested.

Josiah was lying on his bed thinking about the dragon problem when he heard the sound of wings outside his solar. Seconds later the dragon burst through his window with a rush of cool air. Folding his wings, the creature perched in the window opening. "You can't stay there," Josiah said sternly. "Someone will see you."

"This window faces the sea," the dragon reminded him in its childish voice. "Your fears are groundless."

"Well, I still don't like you perching in the window like that," the young prince retorted crossly.

The dragon hopped down upon the floor.

"You were too obvious today," Josiah accused. "My friend Selwyn saw you flying over the forest. You can't let people spot you. If you keep flying in and out of my window, folks will see you and know that I am keeping a dragon. You don't understand how much trouble it would create for me. And I really don't think it is a good idea to keep you here in the solar—someone could open the door unexpectedly and see you. "

"That's not a problem," the creature returned.

"That's easy for you to say," Josiah replied hotly. "I'm the one who will get in trouble if anyone associates you with me."

"It's still not a problem," the dragon insisted. "Should anyone enter the solar, I would simply—"

Josiah stared. The spot where the dragon had stood was now empty. He turned and quickly scanned the room. "All right, where are you?"

"Right here where you saw me last," the dragon replied. The creature slowly materialized right where it had been before, laughing at the look of astonishment that had appeared on Josiah's face. "I won't give you away. If you ever have unexpected visitors, I'll make myself scarce. Nay, my prince, you need not worry about me."

The dragon eyed the game bag. "What did you bring me?" Without a word, Josiah emptied the sack, tossing the four carcasses to the creature.

The evening meal in the great hall of the Castle of Faith was always a festive occasion, one which Prince Josiah ordinarily looked forward to. The castle residents would gather not only to partake of the King's bounty, but also to exchange bits of news, to encourage and exhort each other, and to praise their King. The meal was a time of music, of laughter, of fellowship. It was a time to refresh one's soul and bask in the goodness of King Emmanuel.

Prince Josiah reached the door of the great hall and turned to wait for Gilda and Selwyn. In a moment he saw them hurrying across the bailey. "Have you been waiting long?" Gilda asked, as she and her brother ascended the stairs. "We tried to hurry."

"Actually, I just got here," Josiah replied.

The great hall was an immense, open room with a high, expansive ceiling supported by massive beams. At one end of the great hall, a huge hearth blazed brightly with a warm fire. Immense wrought iron chandeliers ablaze with numerous candles hung over the hall from heavy chains. Three rows of long trestle tables flanked by benches occupied the center of the room. The King's table, a long table at right angles to the others, enjoyed a place of prominence in front of the huge fireplace. The table was ornate, set with silver service, and flanked by upholstered chairs in place of benches.

On this evening, knights and their ladies were strolling casually into the great hall, laughing and conversing warmly with each other. Squires and pages called to each other, and children laughed and chattered happily. Ladies-in-waiting exchanged greetings with members of the castle staff while servants and scullions hurried here and there, filling goblets and bearing platters of food. Two minstrels stood near the fireplace playing a cheerful melody on their lutes. In the noisy hustle and bustle of the preparation for the evening meal, the atmosphere in the great hall was one of anticipation, happiness, and contentment.

Prince Josiah and his companions made their way to the King's table. Lord Watchful, Captain Assurance, Captain Diligence, and their ladies joined them at the table. An attendant rang a silver bell, and the castle's residents quickly took their places around their respective tables. A hush fell across the great hall.

Lord Watchful stood to his feet. "We wish to honor our King and show our gratitude for his provision," he announced. The constable held a rolled parchment in his right hand. He opened his hand, and the parchment vanished.

Moments later, attendants swarmed around the tables, bearing platters and chargers and large bowls of food. There were platters of miniature meat pastries, pheasants in cinnamon sauce, beef fritters, eels in spicy puree, loaches in cold green sauce, slices of roast mutton, filets of saltwater fish, and various garden vegetables. The great hall was filled with tantalizing aromas. "I'm hungry tonight," Josiah announced.

"So am I," Gilda replied. "I think the fresh air whetted my appetite."

An attendant rang the silver bell again, and the great hall fell silent. All eyes turned toward the far end of the hall. "My lords and my ladies," the attendant announced in a clear voice that carried across the vast chamber, "Sir Faithful has an announcement of the utmost importance." As the lords and ladies, servants and scullions, pages and squires and knights all watched in silence, the castle steward ascended the steps of the dais and stood beside King Emmanuel's empty throne. He cleared his throat. The silence in the great hall was overwhelming.

Josiah waited anxiously. Something important was at hand, but what could it be?

Sir Faithful stroked his beard as his gaze swept across the silent castle residents. He cleared his throat a second time, and then began to speak. "Lords and ladies, my beloved friends, forgive my intrusion on your meal, but I must bring a certain matter to your attention. I know that you are anxious to partake of King Emmanuel's bounty, so I will not be tedious. I must make you aware of an impending danger. Today I have received several reports of sightings of a dragon in the vicinity of the Castle of Faith."

Exclamations of dismay and disbelief swept across the vastness of the great hall. The huge chamber was abuzz with conversation as the lords and ladies reacted to the announcement. "See!" Selwyn hissed at Josiah. "I told you that I saw a dragon!" Sir Faithful held up one hand for silence.

"There has not been a dragon sighting in this region of Terrestria for many years. Our young friend, Prince Josiah, killed the dragon Authades some distance from here several months ago, but there has not been a dragon sighting in the vicinity of the castle in recent years. I'm sure that you realize the seriousness of the situation. One witness even stated that the dragon in question was a young Cararian Greatwing."

Another wave of noisy exchanges swept across the hall. Sir Faithful again lifted one hand.

"As many of you know, a Cararian Greatwing is the fiercest of dragons, capable of incredible destruction. A full-grown dragon of this variety can attain a wingspan of fifty feet or more. The report that the dragon is a Cararian has not been substantiated, but it behooves all of us to be alert and watchful. The castle guard will be increased, and I am told that Lord

Watchful is taking other appropriate steps to insure your safety. This is not a time for fear, but I did feel that you should be alerted as to the possible danger that the dragon poses."

Sir Faithful smiled. "That's all for now. My lords and my ladies, enjoy your dinner." As the steward stepped from the dais, the great hall exploded with noisy conversation.

"A Cararian Greatwing!" Selwyn exclaimed. "Remember that day several months ago when we saved that cottage in the forest from burning and the peasant offered us a dragon's egg? Didn't he say that it was the egg of a Cararian Greatwing?"

"Maybe the egg has hatched," Gilda suggested.

Josiah snorted. "If you remember, the peasant also told us that the egg was over two hundred years old and that hatching was impossible." He turned to Selwyn. "Did you tell Sir Faithful that you thought you saw a dragon this afternoon?"

Selwyn shook his head. "Nay, but perhaps I should. He approaches our table now."

Josiah grabbed his arm. "If you say anything now, he'll think you're just trying to get attention because of the other reports."

Selwyn nodded. "Perhaps you are right."

The noise in the great hall gradually abated as the castle residents fell to eating the sumptuous feast set before them. Josiah, Gilda, and Selwyn filled their trenchers and began to eat, enjoying the rich and unusual delicacies of the royal feast. The flaky pastries filled with tender venison, the hot, spicy fritters, the steaming vegetables smothered in butter, the succulent slices of mutton—it was indeed a feast fit for a king.

But Josiah was not enjoying the meal. He ate slowly, realizing for the first time the seriousness of the situation. He had hatched a dragon's egg, had introduced a Cararian Greatwing dragon to the Castle of Faith, and in doing so, had placed the castle residents in danger. The dragon was still young, but was growing larger every day. Josiah had tried to rid himself of the beast, but without success. He was beginning to realize that the dragon was a more formidable adversary than he had imagined. He had, indeed, underestimated the dragon.

"What's wrong, Josiah?" Gilda asked. "You're not eating."

Josiah looked at his trencher. The food was appetizing, as it always was at the King's table, but he found that he was no longer hungry. "I fear that the news of the dragon has caused me to lose my appetite," he replied. "Perhaps I shall just return to my solar. Good night."

The sky was dark the next afternoon as Prince Josiah rode from the castle to take the falcon hunting on the moors. Storm clouds hung low in the heavens and a gusting wind shrieked and howled as it played with the fallen leaves, swirling them around and making them dance in tight circles. An occasional bolt of lightning split the leaden sky, followed by booming reports of thunder that echoed across the moors.

Sir Diligence met him in the steep lane leading from the main gate. "It's not a good day for a hunt, is it, my lord?" the knight called, leaning into the wind as he spoke. "I think I'd rather stay inside the castle."

"Aye, sire, but the falcon needs to be hunted," Josiah replied. "I dare say that we will not stay out long today, though. It looks as if a storm is about to break upon us."

"Stay close to the castle," Sir Diligence suggested, "just in case you get caught in a downpour and have to make a run for it." Spurring his horse forward, he rode across the drawbridge and the young prince continued down the lane.

Upon reaching the moors, Josiah unhooded the falcon and

attached the jesses to her legs. The wind shrieked like a banshee. "It's not a good day for a hunt, girl," he said to Lightning. "I don't see how you can fly against this wind, and you can't go very high or you'll be lost in the clouds, but let's see how you do." He released the falcon.

Lightning shot from his glove like an arrow, climbed to about a hundred feet and then circled the moor. Josiah rode forward, hoping to flush game for the falcon. As he rode through a shallow draw, a hart burst from a thicket and bounded across the moor in huge leaps. "You're a little too big for my falcon to handle," Josiah called to the hart. "Be thankful."

As the mare forded a shallow stream, Josiah heard a loud, raucous screech. He looked skyward just in time to see a dark shape plunge from the clouds and dive straight toward the falcon. "Lightning!" he screamed.

Feathers flew as the enormous predator seized the falcon in its powerful talons. Huge wings beat the air. The hunter and the hunted vanished into the swirling clouds. Josiah sat limp in the saddle. The horrifying scene he had just witnessed had taken place in the barest fraction of a second, but he knew exactly what had happened. The dragon had killed his falcon.

Chapter Thirteen

Prince Josiah sat silently on the edge of his bed, stunned by the sudden loss of the magnificent peregrine falcon. The cage stood empty, a silent reminder of the horror that he had just witnessed, while the falcon's hood and lure lay on the floor nearby. Rage flooded through his soul like a surging river overflowing its banks at flood stage. The dragon knew that the falcon belonged to him—killing his pet was an act of defiance that would not go unpunished.

He drew the book from within his doublet, swung it to transform it into his sword, and then carefully placed the weapon upon the bed beside him. He would have his revenge. The instant the dragon made its appearance, Josiah would drive the sword through its heart. It was something he should have done long ago.

"Lightning." He said the falcon's name and found himself struggling to control his emotions. The magnificent peregrine had belonged to him for just a few short weeks, but he suddenly realized just how much the falcon had meant to him. The unexpected loss left an empty void within his heart. Never again would he hunt the moors, never again would he thrill to watch Lightning dive from the heights in a breath-taking stoop. His rage against the dragon increased.

The dragon. If I had never brought the dragon's egg into the castle, Lightning would still be alive. The thought haunted him. The dragon's egg, an act of disobedience against his King, had already cost him far more than he would ever have imagined. *If only I had never returned to the cottage for another look at the egg.*

He picked up the sword. He would be ready. The moment the wretched beast flew through the window, one thrust of the invincible sword would end its life forever. He sighed. How much easier it would have been when the dragon was first hatched. Already the creature was as tall as he was, with a wingspan approaching twelve feet. At the present rate of growth, in another day or two the dragon would no longer fit through the window of the solar.

Josiah glanced at the empty cage. How would he explain the falcon's death to Selwyn and Gilda? What would he say to Sir Faithful? He fingered the sharp blade of the sword. What would Sir Dither say when he learned that his beloved falcon had been killed?

Darkness descended upon the land of Terrestria, but the young prince did not light a lamp. A small amount of light came through the window; he would be able to make out the silhouette of the dragon when its body entered the window. If the solar were dark and the dragon could not see him, the element of surprise would give him an advantage.

He waited in the darkness for hours, his sword at the ready just inches from his knee. Finally, overcome with exhaustion, he lay down for a moment. The dragon was taking so long to return to the castle...

The morning sun reflected off the waters of the Bay of Opportunity, brightening the solar with its rays. Josiah rubbed his eyes and rolled over. His elbow struck the sword. The feel of the cold steel jerked him awake and he sat up, yawning. The dragon! Gripping the sword, he leaped from the bed and scanned the chamber, but there was no sign of the creature. To his surprise, the dragon had not returned during the night.

Holding the sword against his side, he transformed it into the book. His heart ached as he thought about the loss of his beloved falcon. He avoided looking at the cage as he dressed quickly for breakfast.

His heart was heavy as he descended the stairs and crossed the bailey to the great hall. Selwyn and Gilda waited for him at the door. "Good morning, Josiah," Gilda greeted him cheerfully. "How are you this morning?"

Josiah forced a smile. "I'm fine, Gilda. And I trust that you are, too."

"Gilda and I wanted to go with you this afternoon when you hunt the falcon," Selwyn told him. "Would you like some company on the hunt?"

Josiah shook his head. "There won't be any more hunts, Selwyn." He bit his lip. He might as well tell Selwyn and get it over with. "Lightning is dead."

"Dead?" The brother and sister both stared at him in shock. "What happened?"

"I was hunting her out on the moors yesterday afternoon. The—the dragon came and killed her."

"Oh, Josiah," Gilda said softly.

"The dragon? Are you sure?" Selwyn's face reflected his astonishment.

Josiah nodded. "I saw it happen."

"Oh, Josiah, I'm sorry," Gilda said immediately, her eyes filling with tears. "She was such a magnificent bird, and I know you loved her dearly."

Selwyn touched his arm. "I'm sorry to hear it, Josiah. What happened?"

Josiah took a deep breath. "Yesterday it was really cloudy and windy, remember? Lightning was circling the moor, just about a hundred feet in the air. She couldn't go too much higher, or she would have been in the clouds where she couldn't see a thing. All of a sudden, the dragon dived from the clouds and snatched her in its talons. I—I saw it happen."

The brother and sister again expressed their regrets. "I thank you," Josiah said, struggling with his emotions. "Lightning was a magnificent bird, and her loss will weigh upon my heart. There will never be another falcon quite like her."

"Are you going to get another?" Gilda asked softly.

Josiah shook his head. "I don't know."

"What are you going to do with her cage and stuff?"

"I may keep it in my solar for awhile; I may put it up in the loft over the stables so that it doesn't remind me of her. I haven't decided yet."

Gilda smiled at him and took his hand. "Let's go get breakfast, shall we?"

As they dined at the King's table, Selwyn glanced at Sir Faithful and then looked back to Josiah. "You do know that you need to tell Sir Faithful what happened yesterday, do you not?"

Josiah nodded and gave a long sigh. "I suppose I do. I'll tell him right after breakfast."

"I am sorry, Josiah," the old steward said as the three young people told him the story of the dragon's attack on the falcon. He looked grave. "This makes the situation even more perilous. If this beast had the courage to attack the falcon in your presence, that tells us that it has very little fear of humans. We can only guess what will happen next, but it might not be too much longer before it starts attacking people."

He turned to Josiah. "Was it the same dragon that others have reported seeing? A young one?"

The young prince nodded. "I think so. It was not nearly as large as Authades. I suppose that it had a twelve-foot wingspan."

Sir Faithful seemed relieved. "Let us hope it is the same one. We don't need two of these vile beasts threatening the safety of our people." He snapped his fingers as an idea suddenly occurred to him. "Would you three run an errand for me? Immediately?"

"Anything, sire," Selwyn responded.

"Ride into the Village of Dedication for me," the steward said, stroking his beard thoughtfully. "Find the reeve and have him warn the residents of the village. Tell him that there is no need to sound an alarm, but that the townspeople ought to know what we are facing. I'll also send messengers to some of the other towns around."

"A young Cararian Greatwing, you say?" The reeve seemed incredulous. "Are you certain, my lord?"

"Nobody knows for certain that it is a Cararian Greatwing, sir," Selwyn replied, "but there have been several sightings, and the creature is definitely a dragon. It attacked Josiah's falcon while he was hunting yesterday, and Sir Faithful says that is a sign that it may attack humans before long. He just wanted you to alert the townspeople."

The reeve shook his head. "I just can't believe it. Do you know how long ago we had the last dragon sighting in this region of Terrestria? It's been years and years, so long ago that I really don't remember what year." He looked from one young person to another. "Does Sir Faithful have any idea where the creature might have come from?"

"He didn't say, sir."

"And all the sightings were by residents of the Castle of Faith, close to the castle?"

"Aye, sir," Selwyn responded. "Except that Josiah was out on the moors when the dragon attacked his falcon."

The reeve turned to Josiah. "How far were you from the castle when the dragon attacked, my lord?"

"Not more than two or three furlongs, sir. I was east of the village."

The reeve pursed his lips, deep in thought. "So all of the sightings have been rather close to the Castle of Faith," he said slowly, "while none of the townspeople have reported seeing anything. That tells me that something or someone is drawing the dragon to the castle."

"Sir Faithful suggests that you alert the townspeople, sir," Josiah told the reeve, "but at this point he sees no need to sound a general alarm."

The man nodded. "I agree. Please tell Sir Faithful that I will alert my people. And I thank you, my lords and my lady, for bringing me the message."

Ten minutes later, the three young messengers rode up the lane leading to the main gate of the castle. "Look, Josiah," Selwyn called, pointing toward the battlements of the castle walls. "I have never seen so many sentries! Lord Watchful has put the castle on high alert! I wonder what has happened."

"The sentries are all watching the sky," Gilda observed. "This has something to do with the dragon."

Josiah reined to a stop as they entered the gatehouse area. "Why is the castle on high alert?" he asked a knight standing guard. "What has happened?"

"The dragon has returned, my lord," the knight replied. "Less than half an hour ago it attacked a sentry atop the wall!"

"How did it happen?" Selwyn queried.

"The creature just dropped out of the sky and struck one of the sentries from behind," the knight answered. "He managed to draw his sword, but on the second pass the dragon knocked him from the wall."

"Was he badly hurt?" Gilda asked.

"Aye, my lady, but he's in the castle infirmary right now and they say he will recover. Lord Watchful has sent a petition to His Majesty, King Emmanuel, informing him of the attack."

King Emmanuel! Josiah's heart pounded. Now His Majesty knew about the dragon.

Josiah stood on the sentry walk atop the northern wall of the Castle of Faith. The wind howled around the corners and towers of the castle. The moors and the forest were blanketed in white, the first snow of the season. It had been three days now since he had last seen the dragon in his solar—perhaps the creature was nesting in the forest. If he could find its lair and destroy it, life in the castle would return to normal.

Peering through the brass spyglass that Lord Watchful had loaned him, the young prince carefully scanned the moors for any sign of the dragon. Nothing was moving. He turned his attention to the forest. After several minutes of searching, he carefully set the spyglass in one of the crenels. From this vantage, he could find no sign of the dragon in the forest.

Moments later he caught a glimpse of a dark shape gliding above the forest. His heart leaped. When he put the spyglass to his eye, he was disappointed to learn that it was just a hawk. He quickly searched the forest and the moors again, but there was still no sign of the dragon.

He frowned. Three days. Was it possible that the dragon had left the region? Could it be that he was finally free of the wretched creature? It was too much to hope for. The dragon would not leave that easily—it would have to be driven off or killed. Josiah was beginning to suspect that since he was the one responsible for bringing the beast to the Castle of Faith, he would have to be the one to destroy it.

"Lord Watchful!" The shout came from the sentry in the southeast tower. "Sire, the dragon approaches the castle!"

Josiah whirled around. Two furlongs away, high in the heavens, a large, dark shape was winging its way westward toward the Castle of Faith. The young prince knew even before he lifted the spyglass that the winged creature approaching the castle was the dreaded Cararian Greatwing dragon. Fear swept over him like a cold wind from the north.

The walls of the Castle of Faith suddenly swarmed with armed knights. Lord Watchful dashed up the stairs and ran across the sentry walk to the guard post directly above the gatehouse. "Where is the dragon?"

Several knights pointed at the same time. "Yonder, my lord."

Lord Watchful studied the approaching dragon for a long moment. "Archers, at the ready!" he called. Archers with longbows took positions on the battlements, arrows in place upon the bowstrings, ready to go to full draw as the creature came closer. Not a word was spoken. It was as if the castle itself was waiting with bated breath.

Josiah dropped to one knee on the sentry walk, looking skyward with a fearful eye. Was the dragon actually about to attack the castle? What if it spotted him? Would it attack him? Or would it do something to betray him to the castle inhabitants as the one responsible for bringing it in the first place? He waited anxiously.

Now high in the heavens directly above the Castle of Faith, the dragon circled the castle on motionless wings. Tension mounted. Faces turned skyward, the two garrisons of knights silently followed the dragon as it soared across the heavens.

A woman shrieked with fear. Lord Watchful glanced down and noticed that the west bailey was filling with servants and residents of the castle. Eyes wide, they stood motionless with gaping mouths as they watched the approaching dragon. "Women and children inside!" the constable barked. "Now!" The spectators scattered like dry leaves driven by a north wind.

A raucous screech resounded across the heavens. Immediately every eye jumped back to the soaring dragon. The creature abruptly folded its wings and dropped from the heavens, streaking toward the castle in a breath-taking dive. Stalwart knights trembled. "Archers, take aim!" Lord Watchful called. As one, the archers drew their bowstrings back until the feathers of the fletching touched their right cheeks. The muscles in their brawny arms stood out as the archers stood at full draw, ready to release their arrows upon command.

The sound of steel echoed across the bailey as swords were drawn. The Castle of Faith waited in breathless silence.

Faster and faster, the speeding dragon plummeted toward the castle wall. Fear tore at Josiah's heart. The dreaded creature was heading straight for him! He raised his sword with a trembling hand.

"Archers, release!" At the sharp twang of the bowstrings, a score of arrows leaped from the archers' bows. The barrage of arrows sped through the air, striking the dragon in the region of its heart. To the dismay of those who watched, the missiles were deflected and fell harmlessly to the bailey below. Screeching hideously, the huge beast struck the edge of the battlements with its talons, and then, with a mighty downbeat of its enormous wings, rose in the air. Another barrage of arrows followed it futilely.

"Did you see the size of that creature?" one knight called incredulously.

"Twenty-five feet from wingtip to wingtip, at the very least," another replied.

"Aye, the beast is growing rapidly," a third responded. "It is far larger than when I saw it the other day."

As they watched, the dragon climbed higher and higher in the heavens, circled the castle twice, and then winged its way north above the forest. Josiah found it in the spyglass. Just as he did, the creature suddenly spiraled downward into the forest. The young prince caught his breath. Apparently, the dragon *was* nesting in the forest!

"My lord, allow me to take my garrison and follow the beast," Sir Dedication called out. "We shall track it to its lair and destroy it."

"Nay, Sir Dedication," Lord Watchful replied. "The castle is better served if your men stay here and defend it."

Josiah was already hurrying down the stairs. The drawbridge was still down, the portcullis was up, and the gate was still open. In the excitement of watching the attack from the air, the castle defenders had neglected to secure the main gate of the castle. The young prince slipped through unnoticed.

He alone was responsible for bringing the Cararian Greatwing to the Castle of Faith, and he knew deep in his heart that only he could stop it. He had fought a dragon before—a full-grown, experienced dragon far larger and more powerful than this fledgling. When he had fought the dragon Authades, victory had come only after a great struggle, but he had won the victory. Cararian Greatwing or not, this dragon was barely half-grown. Young and inexperienced, it would be no match for the power of King Emmanuel's invincible sword. He, Prince Josiah, would save the Castle of Faith from the airborne menace.

The snow crunched under his sabotons as he marched resolutely toward the forest where the young Cararian Greatwing lurked. Behind him stretched a double line of footprints in the snow.

Chapter Fourteen

Prince Josiah stood at the edge of the snowy forest, silently surveying the path before him. His breath hung like a cloud in the frigid air. From the castle wall he had seen the dragon drop into the forest at a point less than four furlongs from the castle, and he remembered that there was a small meadow in that vicinity where he had often hunted with Lightning. He decided to hike to that location and commence his search for the dragon from the meadow.

His sabotons made a pleasant crunching sound in the snow as he hurried through the forest. An ice storm had swept over the forest the night before, magically transforming the trees into mysterious sculptures of sparkling crystal. The morning sun glistened on the new-fallen snow with a brilliance that hurt the eyes while millions of brilliant diamonds seemed to dance and shimmer in the drifts around him. A fallen log lying across the trail was festooned with a row of glistening icicles. In spite of the cold, the scene before him was a fantasy land of breath-taking beauty.

He drew his sword. The cold steel felt good in his hand. "Wretched beast," he said aloud, "you have killed my falcon and attacked my castle. Prepare to die, for you shall soon taste the steel of my sword. When I find you, I shall drive the blade of this mighty weapon through your vile heart!"

His own heart pounded at the prospect of coming face to face with the dragon. No longer the helpless, trembling hatchling that had first emerged from the egg, the dragon was now a half-grown Cararian Greatwing, capable of striking fear into the hearts of the stoutest of men. Josiah had witnessed the incredible power of the great wings, the enormous talons that could tear a knight limb from limb, the powerful tail capable of smashing the sturdiest armor. He had no doubt that a Cararian Greatwing, even a half-grown one, would prove to be a formidable adversary.

But he was not afraid. He carried the invincible sword designed by King Emmanuel himself. Had he not wielded it in battle against the great dragon Authades? Had he not emerged the victor from the dragon's lair? This conflict would be no different—Cararian Greatwing or no, by nightfall the dragon would be dead.

Moments later Prince Josiah entered the meadow. Sheets of ice like panes of glass lined the banks of a small, winding creek. A rabbit hopped from its burrow, paused and looked at him tentatively, and then hopped on about its business. He paused at the edge of the stream and studied the meadow. There were no tracks: nothing to indicate that the dragon had passed that way.

Leaping across the tiny stream, he skirted the edge of the meadow and entered the forest on the other side. His senses were keenly alert as he scanned the area for his adversary. There was still no sign of the dragon, but he slowly became aware of a nagging sensation of danger. He felt as if he was being watched. Gripping his sword tightly, he turned about in a slow circle, carefully studying the forest around him.

The dragon was nowhere to be seen, but the young prince still couldn't dismiss the uneasy feeling inside. He couldn't explain it, but something inside told him that he was in great danger. He took a deep breath.

"Prince Josiah," a low voice called, "why do you seek me with a sword in your hand?" The arrogant, childish voice had been replaced by the deeper voice of a youth, but there was no mistaking the voice of the dragon.

Moving only his eyes, Josiah carefully scanned the forest around him. As yet he had no idea as to the location of the dragon. "I seek you that I might destroy you," he replied, trying to keep his voice from trembling. He turned his head slightly, still searching for his adversary.

"Why do you seek to destroy me?" The dragon sounded as if it were slightly amused.

"You killed my falcon," Josiah replied angrily. "Lightning was special to me and you knew it, yet you destroyed her."

"The bird was claiming too much of your time," the unseen creature explained in a slightly conciliatory tone. "I had to remove her so that you would have time for me."

"I want nothing to do with you!" Josiah stormed. "Before I leave this forest today, I intend to slay you."

The dragon sighed. "I have plans for you, my prince. I can bring you thrills and pleasures such as you have never known, yet you seek to destroy me."

"You attacked the castle and injured a friend of mine," Josiah accused hotly. "I should never have brought you into the Castle of Faith in the first place, for that was a violation of King Emmanuel's royal law." Out of the corner of his eye, he detected a slight movement and turned in that direction. The image disappeared. Turning his head back, he again looked out of the corner of his eye and could just make out a large, indistinct outline. Raising his sword, he moved cautiously toward it.

"Take care, foolish prince," the creature warned. "You do not realize what a Cararian Greatwing is capable of. My scales can turn the sharpest arrows and blunt the strongest spears. I can tear you in pieces as easily as a housecat would devour a sparrow. If you are wise, you will simply retrace your steps and return to the castle."

"I am not afraid of you," Josiah retorted. "I am armed with the invincible sword of King Emmanuel." He continued to move forward.

"Such a weapon is powerless in the hands of the likes of you," the creature sneered.

"This sword embodies the power of King Emmanuel," the young prince declared. "I have already used it to slay one dragon, and today I shall slay another."

The dragon abruptly appeared before him, and Prince Josiah gasped as he realized just how formidable an adversary he faced. The monster was now fully twenty-five feet long, with scaly, green hide and enormous, bat-like wings. Its head was immense, with huge, dark eyes that smoldered with fire and a cavernous mouth with rows of wicked- looking teeth. The dragon's enormous legs terminated in claws that looked as if they could tear through the strongest armor. The odor of decaying flesh engulfed the creature.

"Return to the castle, foolish prince," the dragon raged, "or I shall leave your carcass to rot in the forest. I warn you, if you try to destroy me, I will kill you. You have never seen the destruction that a Cararian Greatwing is capable of wreaking."

"Never again shall you attack the Castle of Faith or take that which belongs to me," Josiah cried, leaping over an ice-coated log and charging directly at the dragon. He hit a patch of ice and his feet shot out from under him, landing him flat on his back at the feet of the dragon. His sword landed in a snowdrift beside him.

"Foolish prince," the dragon roared, pinning Josiah to the ground with one huge claw. "Already I have you in my power and I can crush you like a worm, should I so choose."

Josiah struggled to breathe. The terrible weight of the dragon pinned him to the earth, crushing the breath out of him. His lungs screamed for air. A horrible blackness descended before his eyes, threatening to engulf him.

"Return to the castle," the dragon commanded again, "or I shall end your miserable life here and now." Suddenly the pressure on Josiah's chest ceased as the dragon lifted its claw.

The young prince lay still for a moment, gulping huge lungfuls of air. Slowly he stood to his feet. Seeing the handle of his sword protruding from the snowdrift, he seized it with both hands and whirled about, swinging the invincible weapon with all his might.

To Josiah's amazement, the dragon was no longer there. An immense shadow loomed over him and he looked up to see the creature hovering fifty feet in the air. "My patience is at an end, foolish prince," the beast roared. "You insist on attacking me, so now I must destroy you."

The dragon abruptly swooped down, striking Josiah squarely in the chest and knocking him backward in the snow. Josiah managed to maintain his grip on the sword. He rolled to his feet, gripping the weapon with both hands. Twenty feet to his left, the dragon calmly waited for him. Josiah raised the sword.

The dragon's tail slammed into him with all the force of a battering ram, sending him sprawling and knocking the sword from his hands. Josiah lay motionless in the snow, dazed and struggling to breathe. Snorting with rage, the dragon slowly advanced toward the fallen prince. Desperately, Josiah crawled forward. His hands probed the snow as he frantically searched for the lost weapon.

He felt a crushing pressure on his chest and back as the dragon seized him in its teeth, shook him furiously, and hurled him across the clearing to land like a crumpled rag doll against the base of a rock ledge. The forest seemed to spin crazily in a blurring confusion of white. The dragon roared mightily, and Josiah's heart constricted with fear. Through the fog of his pain and confusion he saw a narrow space beneath the ledge and managed to crawl into it. The throbbing in his head increased to an unbearable pitch, and darkness descended suddenly.

Josiah awoke to find that he was back in his solar in the Castle of Faith. Selwyn and Gilda stood at the foot of his bed, looking at him anxiously. "How—how did I get here?" Josiah asked.

"One of the sentries saw your footprints leading into the forest," Selwyn explained. "A detail of knights tracked you into the forest and found you unconscious beneath a rock ledge. They brought you here."

"Did—did they see the dragon?" the young prince asked anxiously.

"Nay, but they saw plenty of evidence that he had been there," his friend replied. "They said that the ground was torn up as if there had been a tremendous struggle. The earth at the base of the ledge was dug up where the dragon had tried to get at you, but couldn't."

"Why did you try to fight the dragon yourself?" Gilda asked, with a worried look creasing her pretty face. "You could have been killed."

Josiah didn't attempt to explain.

Sir Faithful entered the solar just then. "You're awake," he greeted Josiah. "How are you feeling?"

"My head hurts," Josiah replied, sitting up, "but I think I'm all right otherwise."

"You should never have gone after that dragon by yourself," the steward scolded, shaking his head. "Lad, you were facing a Cararian Greatwing! Do you not realize what that beast could have done to you?"

Josiah grimaced. "I found out, sire."

"Nay, it could have done far worse. A Cararian Greatwing is no adversary to be taken lightly. Next time, inform me before you try such a stunt."

The young prince nodded.

"Get some rest," Sir Faithful said gently. "I'll send a page at dinner time to see if you feel like coming to dinner in the great hall." He motioned to Gilda and Selwyn. "Come on, let's allow this foolhardy young prince to get some rest."

A loud knock at the door woke Josiah instantly. He swung his feet over the side of the bed and stood slowly. The solar floor seemed to sway beneath his feet and he grabbed the bedpost to steady himself. Walking slowly and unsteadily, he made his way to the door.

To his surprise, the door opened to reveal the unsmiling face of the castle constable. One look at his countenance and the young prince could tell that something was amiss. "Lord Watchful," Josiah said uneasily, "is something wrong?"

"Come with me, Prince Josiah," the constable said sternly. "Sir Faithful requests your presence in the great hall."

A cold apprehension swept over Josiah as he followed Lord Watchful down the stairs, across the bailey, and into the great hall. Usually warm and friendly, the constable was stern and distant, and Josiah could tell by his demeanor that something serious was about to happen. They entered the great hall to find the vast chamber filled with the castle residents. A steely silence fell over the assembly as Josiah entered. Tension filled the air. Lord Watchful led Josiah to the far end of the great hall, where Sir Faithful stood waiting on the raised dais.

The look on the steward's face was one that Josiah would never forget. Stroking his long beard, Sir Faithful gazed at him sadly for a long moment without speaking. Josiah thought he detected a note of disappointment in the old man's eyes. Nervously, he cleared his throat. "You—you sent for me, sire?"

"Prince Josiah," the old man said slowly, reluctantly, "my heart rejoiced when you became a member of His Majesty's family and came to live in the Castle of Faith. I have watched you learn and grow, and I have seen you serve your King with the zeal and enthusiasm of youth. I have rejoiced with you in your triumphs and wept with you in your losses. In truth, I have loved you as if you were my own son."

He paused and regarded Josiah with sad eyes. "My son, I ask you to tell me the truth, even though I fear that the answer may break my heart." He paused, took a deep breath, and then motioned to a servant standing nearby. "Josiah, where did this come from?" The servant stepped forward and handed an object to Sir Faithful. Exclamations of surprise swept across the great hall.

Josiah's heart seemed to stop. The steward was holding a large fragment of eggshell, nearly six inches long and two inches wide. "One of the servants gave this to me this very afternoon. He found it beneath your bed when he changed the reeds on the floor of your solar. Josiah, what can you tell me about this?"

Silence reigned in the great hall. Josiah stared at the piece of eggshell. He began to tremble. When he opened his mouth to speak, no words came out.

"This fragment is from the eggshell of a Cararian Greatwing dragon," Sir Faithful said quietly, though his voice resounded across the vast chamber. "Possession of a dragon or a dragon's egg is expressly forbidden under royal law, yet we found this in your solar. Josiah, did you bring the egg of a Cararian Greatwing into the Castle of Faith?"

The tension in the great hall was like a moment of calm before the onset of a fierce thunderstorm. Not a soul moved or spoke. Time seemed to stand still.

"Prince Josiah, did you or did you not bring a dragon's egg into the castle?"

Josiah nodded miserably. The terrible secret, that which he had guarded so carefully, was finally out. In that dreadful moment, every soul within the Castle of Faith learned that he had disobeyed King Emmanuel's royal law and brought a dragon's egg into the castle. He bowed his head in shame.

Murmurs of astonishment and indignation echoed across the great hall.

"Did that egg hatch in your solar?"

Again, Josiah nodded. His face burned with shame.

"And is that dragon the very one which has been sighted in the vicinity of the Castle of Faith, the one which has on two occasions attacked the castle?"

The young prince took a deep breath. "Aye, sire."

Sir Faithful's face was stern. "So, Josiah, you are the one

responsible for bringing the treacherous Cararian Greatwing dragon to the Castle of Faith, thus endangering the castle residents?"

Josiah swallowed hard. "Aye, sire," he replied weakly.

The elderly steward bowed his head. For several long moments he seemed to study the stones in the floor. When he raised his head, his eyes were filled with tears. "My son, do you not understand the seriousness of what you have done?"

The young prince couldn't answer.

"A Cararian Greatwing is the fiercest of all dragons," Sir Faithful said quietly. "By bringing the dragon to the Castle of Faith you endangered the lives of everyone within the castle, and brought dishonor to the name of His Majesty. My son, how could you do such a thing?"

"S—Selwyn and Gilda and I saved a peasant's cottage from burning to the ground," Josiah stammered feebly. "He and his wife offered us the egg as a reward, but we refused. On the day that I rode to the Castle of Steadfastness, I stopped by the cottage on the return trip, just for a brief look at the egg. The peasant offered me the egg again, sire, and I—I accepted." He spread his hands wide as if to make an appeal. "He told me that the egg was dead and would never hatch."

"Did you know that the egg was that of a Cararian Greatwing, the egg of a dragon?" Lord Watchful asked sternly.

Josiah couldn't bring himself to look at the constable. "Aye, sire," he whispered miserably.

"Speak up, my prince," Lord Watchful demanded.

"Aye, sire, I did."

"Were you aware of the fact that possession of such an egg was in direct violation of His Majesty's royal decrees?"

"Aye, sire." Josiah made a feeble attempt at defending his actions. "When I went back to the cottage, sire, I did not intend to take the egg. I—I merely wanted another look at it. The—the peasant talked me into taking it."

"So this whole matter is the peasant's fault."

"Aye, sire, I suppose it is—nay, sire! I am the one at fault. But after I realized what I had done, I took the egg to the forest to destroy it. I tried, sire, I really did. But I found that I simply could not do it."

Sir Faithful and Lord Watchful frowned and looked at each other. The castle residents waited in stunned silence. At last, the steward spoke. "Prince Josiah, what do you have to say for yourself?"

Josiah dropped his head. "Nothing, sire."

"Josiah, you have deliberately defied a royal edict from King Emmanuel himself. You have just acknowledged that you knew the egg to be that of a Cararian Greatwing, and that possession of such was a violation of royal law. By bringing the egg of a Cararian Greatwing into the Castle of Faith, you have dishonored His Majesty's name and placed the Castle of Faith in grave danger."

He paused. "Such a deed must be dealt with in such a way that you will realize that this must never happen again." He turned to Lord Watchful. "Have two of your knights escort Josiah outside the great hall while we discuss this and reach a decision as to how we shall deal with this matter."

All eyes were on Prince Josiah as he walked from the great hall in the company of two knights, his head bowed. An overwhelming sense of shame burned within him. Every soul within the Castle of Faith now knew that he was the one responsible for the Cararian Greatwing dragon, and that he had disobeyed the will of King Emmanuel. Even His Majesty knew, and the thought was almost more than the young prince could bear.

Chapter Fifteen

"Prince Josiah," Sir Faithful said sternly, as the young prince stood apprehensively before him again, "because of your willful disobedience to His Majesty's royal law, the Castle of Faith is now threatened by a fierce Cararian Greatwing dragon. You have admitted that you brought the egg into the castle, and that you were fully aware that the egg was that of a dragon, expressly forbidden by His Majesty, King Emmanuel. Yet you have shown little remorse.

"Your actions have jeopardized the safety of the castle residents. Disobedience to His Majesty always brings serious consequences, both to you personally and to those around you. As the steward of the castle, I am charged with the responsibility of seeing that you face personal consequences." He sighed. "Josiah, you are hereby forbidden to enter the great hall of the Castle of Faith until further notice. You will take your meals alone in your solar. Your food will be delivered to you at the regular times."

"I'm being banished to my solar, sire?"

"Furthermore, at this time you are also being relieved of your regular duties of service to Emmanuel. Possession of the egg, and of the dragon, has rendered you ineffective in

His Majesty's service. To allow you to ride into battle in His Majesty's name would jeopardize the lives of others."

Josiah raised his eyes. "I—I can no longer serve King Emmanuel?" Tears threatened, and he struggled to hold them back. "Sire, why can I not serve my King?"

"Your heart is not yielded to the will of Emmanuel," the old steward answered sadly. "To attempt to serve Emmanuel at this time would be ineffectual at best, and quite possibly dangerous to others. Your disobedience in bringing the dragon's egg to the castle has rendered you unfit for His Majesty's service."

He paused. "Later this evening we will observe the King's Supper in the great hall, but you will not be present. Your heart is not prepared to commemorate Emmanuel's sacrifice for you."

Josiah's heart cried out at these words. The King's Supper, a simple meal of unleavened bread and juice from the fruit of the vine, was a sacred event when the castle residents gathered to commemorate King Emmanuel's death for them. The juice, symbolic of the King's blood, and the bread, symbolic of his body, reminded them of the tremendous sacrifice their sovereign had made when he purchased their freedom. The King's Supper was a sacred time, a blessed time, but tonight, Josiah would miss it.

The young prince struggled to control his emotions. He tried to speak, but could not. At last, he simply bowed his head.

"Return to your solar, Josiah," Sir Faithful ordered quietly. "The evening meal in the great hall will proceed without you."

Devastated by the steward's words, Josiah walked slowly from the great hall in utter shame. He glanced at Selwyn and Gilda as he passed the King's table. Both of his friends flashed him looks of sorrow and then looked away quickly. The loneliness in his heart increased until he thought he would be unable to bear the pain. His chest tightened. He struggled to breathe.

The door of the great hall slammed shut behind him with a heavy thud that resounded across the west bailey. His heart was heavy as he trudged across the bailey, alone. The evening meal in the great hall had always been his favorite time of the entire day—it was a joyful, contented time of fellowship, feasting at the King's table, and praising the name of Emmanuel. And tonight he would miss it. A lump grew in his throat.

He thought about the King's Supper. What a blessed time as the castle residents commemorated the sacrifice of their King. He sighed heavily. Tonight he would miss it.

If only I had known how much trouble the dragon's egg would cause, he thought sorrowfully as he climbed the stairs toward his solar in the northwest tower, *I never, never would have brought it into the Castle of Faith. I wish that I had never returned to the peasant's cottage for another look at that wretched egg. Who would have thought that it would ever hatch out a live dragon?*

An intense feeling of loneliness swept over him as he entered his solar. *I wonder what will happen now. Can anyone slay the dragon before it attacks the castle again? I hatched the dragon—what if I am the only one who can slay it? But I have already tried and failed. What if no one can slay it?*

He stepped to the window and looked down at the sea far below, and a new thought suddenly occurred to him. *What if I were to leave the castle? The dragon came to the castle because of me, and perhaps it was seeking me when it attacked. Suppose I were to leave the castle— can I escape the dragon in that way? Or would the dragon follow me? Could I protect the Castle of Faith by drawing the dragon away?*

A knock sounded at the door just then, startling him and interrupting his thoughts. He opened the door to find a young page standing on the sentry walk with a tray of food. "Your meal, sire." The servant handed him the tray and quickly turned away.

Josiah carried the tray inside his solar and lifted the lid. To his disappointment, the meal consisted of a few thin slices of roast mutton, a serving of carrots, and a thick slice of dark bread. "No roast pheasant, or beef pastries, or fancy jellies tonight," he said bitterly. "Tonight I get just enough food to keep me alive." He sighed. "So this is yet another price I must pay for possessing the dragon's egg—I no longer dine at the King's table."

Several minutes later, after finishing the meager meal, he placed the tray outside the door of his solar. The sun had already set, though thin traces of a gold and purple sunset still lingered in the darkening skies. The bailey was dark.

If I leave tonight, I won't be missed until morning, he thought abruptly. *Perhaps I can escape the dragon, but, if not, I will have drawn him away from the Castle of Faith.* He sighed. *I never thought that I would ever want to leave the Castle of Faith, and yet, perhaps it is best. I've endangered the castle and dishonored His Majesty—perhaps my leaving will make up for some of the damage I have caused.*

The moon was just beginning to peek over the eastern walls of the castle as he slipped furtively from his solar, crossed the bailey in the shadows, and approached the small postern gate. He glanced upward. A sentry stood at attention on the sentry walk just above the gate.

Josiah waited and watched from the shadows. Sir Faithful had not said that he could not leave the castle, only that he was not allowed inside the great hall. Would the sentry challenge him if he attempted to open the gate? Was he allowed to leave the castle, or would the sentry stop him? He wasn't sure.

The sentry turned and moved north along the wall. Josiah crept forward silently, crouching in the shadows each time the sentry turned in his direction and moving forward each time he turned away. He gave a sigh of relief when he reached the gate.

His heart pounded madly as he stood to his feet and noiselessly raised the small portcullis and then unbarred the gate. He held his breath and gently pulled the gate open, flinching as the hinges creaked slightly in protest. Without hesitation he slipped from the castle into the night. Glancing upward toward the battlements to ascertain that he was not being observed, he crept silently down the protected walkway toward the sea.

The silver light of the moon danced on the waters of the sea, brightening the bay and adorning each surging breaker with highlights of silver, but in the shadows of the castle, all was dark. Josiah could hear the breakers as they crashed against the rocks at the base of the mighty castle wall, but he could see nothing. He longed for a light. The book! The light from its pages would guide his way. He withdrew the book from within his doublet and opened it eagerly, but to his great disappointment, the pages glowed so feebly that they seemed to be of no use at all. At last, he simply closed the volume and replaced it within his doublet.

He stepped into the cold waters of the bay, and to his surprise, found that they reached only to his waist. *The tide must be out,* he realized gratefully. *When the tide is in the waters would cover my head.* Just then, a powerful wave slammed into him from behind, lifting him off his feet and tumbling him forward toward the beach. He came up coughing and sputtering and struggling to regain his footing.

Moments later the young prince stumbled out onto the sand, thoroughly soaked and exhausted from his ordeal in the surf. He trembled with cold. "I had better walk fast to warm up," he said aloud, "or I shall freeze to death." Glancing over his right shoulder at the moonlit walls of the Castle of Faith, he set out toward the Village of Dedication at a brisk pace.

Half an hour later Josiah topped a small rise and paused to catch his breath. The Village of Dedication was now more than a dozen furlongs behind him. He was making good time, but the cold night air was wearing him down. The plunge into the sea had thoroughly soaked his clothing, and even though he was walking at a brisk pace, he found that he simply could not warm up. The cold of the night was quickly sapping the energy from his body. He knew that he could not go much farther.

He gazed across the peaceful, moonlit valley before him. The moonbeams glistened on the snow and deep purple shadows contrasted with the bright silver of the moonlight, creating a dreamlike fantasyland. He glanced upward. The moon hung low in the heavens, a huge, silver crescent against a backdrop of dark velvet, and seemingly so close that he had to resist the urge to reach up and touch it. Stars twinkled like a king's ransom of diamonds. He shivered. The night was so beautiful, so peaceful, and yet so cold.

A flickering amber light drew his attention to the valley. His heart leaped. A fire! Hardly more than a furlong away, someone had built a campfire. Here was the chance to warm up, to dry out his clothing. The fire would provide a haven from the cold of the night. He hurried toward it with renewed vigor.

Three minutes later Josiah paused and silently surveyed the clearing before him. In the center of a glen ringed with giant oaks, a cheerful fire burned brightly. The flames leaped and danced, throwing unique patterns of light on the trunks of the huge trees. The aroma of roasting meat drew his attention to a wooden spit suspended over the flames on which a roasting pheasant popped and sizzled. Two short logs lay at right angles at a convenient distance from the campfire.

"Halloo, is anyone there?" Josiah called softly, a bit hesitant to step into the clearing. He waited, but there was no answer. "May I take advantage of your campfire?" Still there was no answer.

After waiting in the shadows another moment or two, the young prince crept cautiously forward, drawn by the enticing fire. His heart pounded as he surveyed the clearing before dropping to a seat on one of the logs. Leaning forward, he extended his hands and feet toward the fire, reveling in the warmth from the flames. He glanced downward. An earthenware flask lay at his feet.

The roasting pheasant sizzled enticingly, and the aroma was irresistible. "Your pheasant is roasted to perfection," Josiah said loudly, speaking to the emptiness of the night air. "I'm taking it from the fire for you, rather than letting it burn." There was no answer.

He rubbed his hands together, allowing the warmth from the fire to flow into his fingers, and then he withdrew the spit from the fire. As he did he saw that two apples had been skewered on the stick on either side of the bird, allowing them to roast along with the meat. He rested the stick against the log at an angle so that the golden-brown pheasant wouldn't touch the ground. Bending down, he touched the earthenware flask. It was warm, and felt good to the touch. He lifted it, removed the stopper, and sniffed. The alluring aroma of hot milk filled his nostrils. He replaced the stopper and carefully set the flask in its place at the edge of the fire.

Puzzled, he glanced around the clearing. "It's almost as if I was expected," he said aloud. "It's as if the fire and the food were prepared just for me at a time when I most need them."

He looked around. "I don't know who you are or why you have built this fire and prepared this food," he said loudly, though no one seemed to hear. "If it is for me, I want you to know that I am grateful."

The pheasant and the apples were delicious, and the hot milk provided a golden warmth that seemed to flow throughout his entire being. As he finished the simple meal he yawned drowsily. To his delight, he noticed that a pallet had been spread upon the ground just beyond the fire. Within moments he was fast asleep.

Some time later Josiah awoke with a start. His heart pounded with fear. A dark figure was crouched over the dying embers of the fire. Sparks flew heavenward like golden fireflies as the stranger dropped a stick of wood into the struggling flames. The figure turned, and the young prince gasped. "Sir Wisdom!"

The old nobleman smiled sadly as he extended a hand and touched Josiah's shoulder. "Josiah, my prince, how are you?"

Josiah sat up. "Sire, did you prepare the fire? The pheasant and the apples—were they for me?"

Sir Wisdom nodded. "I knew that you would need them."

Josiah frowned. "But sire, how could you have known? No one knew that I was coming here; I myself did not know."

Sir Wisdom smiled again. "It is my business to know such things, lad."

Josiah yawned. "I still do not understand. How could you possibly know that I would pass by here if I did not even know it myself?"

The old man dropped to a seat on one of the logs. "Tonight you have embarked on a journey, my prince. Do you know where you are going?"

Josiah shook his head. "Nay, not really, sire."

"You are going nowhere, Josiah, for you are attempting to run from a problem, rather than facing it. Running will solve nothing. It will simply delay the inevitable. Cararian Greatwings grow at an alarming rate, and the longer you delay, the greater your adversary will become."

Josiah was alarmed. "Sire, you know about the dragon?"

Sir Wisdom nodded. "The sooner you face the dragon, the better it will be."

A troublesome thought was nagging at Josiah's subconscious. "Does—does King Emmanuel know?"

The nobleman's face was grim. "His Majesty has known all along, my prince. Emmanuel is Lord of all Terrestria. Not a single sparrow falls to the ground but that His Majesty knows all about it."

Josiah was devastated. "Then he knows about the egg, and how I chose to bring it into the castle. He knows that my heart is not yielded..." Troubled, he fell silent.

Sir Wisdom sighed. "Go back to the Castle of Faith, Josiah. There is nothing to be gained by running away."

"Everyone within the castle knows that I am the one responsible for bringing the dragon to the castle," the young prince retorted. "I have been banned from the great hall, excluded from the King's table, cut off from the fellowship that is so dear to me. Why should I go back? There is nothing for me there."

"You must go back and destroy the dragon. That is best done from the safety of the Castle of Faith."

"I have already tried to destroy that vile beast," Josiah said bitterly. "I have tried and failed. I tried to destroy it when it was just an egg, and found that somehow I could not. I tried to stand and fight the dragon, but even though it was only half-grown, I was defeated almost before I started. I cannot return to the castle and destroy the beast; I am powerless before it."

"Why did you try to destroy the egg?" Sir Wisdom asked quietly.

"Sire?" Josiah was puzzled. "I do not understand your question, sire. It was the egg of a Cararian Greatwing; why should I not try to destroy it?"

"And why did you follow the dragon into the forest in an attempt to destroy it?"

"Sire, I do not understand what you are asking. The dragon is a Cararian Greatwing, an adversary of my soul. It was only right that I should try to destroy it; was it not?"

"But *why* did you try to destroy it?" the old man prodded gently. "What was your motivation?"

Josiah shrugged. "I am the son of King Emmanuel," he replied. "His Majesty has forbidden his subjects to possess a dragon, or a dragon's egg; so I was merely attempting to destroy the creature in obedience to the will of His Majesty."

Sir Wisdom looked at him sternly. "Be honest with yourself, my prince, or we will accomplish nothing. If your heart's desire was obedience to the will of His Majesty, you never would have accepted the egg in the first place. Now, again, what was your reason for attempting to destroy the egg, and later, the dragon?"

Prince Josiah sighed. "Perhaps I do not really know, sire."

"Was it not that you were attempting to cover your disobedience—to keep Sir Faithful and the castle residents from finding out that you had brought a dragon's egg into the castle? Your determination to destroy the creature came not from a desire to please His Majesty; rather, it sprang from a desire to conceal your own wrongdoing."

Josiah pondered the nobleman's words. "Is that—is that why I failed? Is that why I found that I could not crush the egg, and why I was powerless when I did face the dragon?"

Sir Wisdom nodded. "Your heart was not yielded to the will of Emmanuel, and therefore you had no power."

Josiah hesitated. "What—what must I do now?"

"Return to the Castle of Faith. Yield your heart to the will of His Majesty. Send a petition acknowledging your wrongdoing and seeking His Majesty's forgiveness. And then, once your heart is fully yielded, seek out the dragon and destroy it."

The young prince shook his head. "I am not yet ready for that. I am not ready to stand before the dragon again."

"The longer you wait, my prince, the more difficult will be your task. The dragon grows larger and fiercer with every passing day."

"I am just not ready."

"I see." The old man surveyed the clearing for a moment and then pointed to a young, two-foot sapling a short distance from the fire. "Do me a favor, my prince. Uproot that sapling for me, would you?"

Josiah shrugged. "Gladly, sire." He strode over, gripped the tiny tree with both hands, and easily pulled it from the soil.

"Aye, my prince, excellent." Sir Wisdom seemed pleased. "Now, permit me one more favor, would you?" He strode across the clearing and placed his hand on the trunk of one of the towering oaks. "Uproot this one for me, would you?"

"Sire, that is impossible. There is not a man in all of Terrestria who could uproot such a mighty oak."

The nobleman shrugged casually. "The sapling was an oak, yet you uprooted it easily. Why can you not do the same with this oak?"

The young prince laughed uneasily, unsure as to where Sir

Wisdom's comments were heading. "This tree is a giant, sire. Uprooting it is an impossibility."

"Years ago this giant was a tiny sapling," Sir Wisdom told him. "At that time, even a child could have uprooted it easily. Now, as you pointed out, the strongest man in all of Terrestria could not move it."

"Sire, what does this have to do with me?"

"You seem content to allow the dragon to exist, although you and I both know that it must be destroyed. It seems that you intend to wait and attempt to destroy it at a later date. But, my prince, Cararian Greatwings grow in size and strength at quite an alarming rate. Today the dragon is barely half-grown, quite a formidable adversary to be sure, but nothing compared to what it will become if you delay. Again, my advice is to return immediately to the Castle of Faith, send a petition of repentance to King Emmanuel, and then destroy the dragon once and for all."

"I am not ready for that, sire."

"Delay will be costly, my prince. You will find yourself attempting to uproot a mighty oak when you could have removed a sapling." He looked Josiah in the eye. "When you faced the young dragon, did it belch fire?"

Josiah thought for a moment. "Nay, sire, I don't believe it did."

"If this Cararian Greatwing is half-grown, as I believe it is, it will soon have that capability, if it does not already. Then you will find yourself facing a truly formidable adversary. I repeat myself, Prince Josiah; you must destroy the beast immediately."

Josiah hesitated. "But, sire, I have tried—"

Sir Wisdom turned and strode across the clearing, calling over his shoulder as he did, "Immediately, my prince. You must destroy the dragon immediately, for delay will prove costly. Good night." Without another word he vanished into the night.

Chapter Sixteen

Prince Josiah awoke to find that the campfire had gone out. The night was still dark. An icy wind howled through the glen, chilling his face and hands and swirling the powdery snow about him in tight little circles. He shivered. He sat up, wrapping the pallet around himself in a futile attempt to stay warm.

He glanced upward. Pale tints of pink and orange were just beginning to glow in the eastern sky, indicating that dawn was not far behind. He yawned and stretched. *If sunrise is less than an hour away I might as well resume my journey rather than staying here and freezing.* He stood and stamped his sabotons in the snow in an effort to warm his cold feet.

Half an hour later the eastern sky had brightened considerably as Josiah found himself passing a quiet farm on the outskirts of a peaceful little village. The baying of a deep-voiced hound announced his passing, and the sound echoed across the hillside. Hearing the flutter of wings overhead, he glanced upward just in time to see an owl alight in a tree and he felt a pang of regret as he thought about his falcon. *That wretched dragon destroyed my beloved pet. If I had not hatched the egg, Lightning would still be alive.* He pushed the thought from his mind and hurried on.

The sun managed to peek over the hills to the east just as Josiah entered the village. He heard a dog yelping in distress and hurried toward the sound. As he rounded the corner of a small shop, a small yelping puppy ran between his feet, nearly knocking him down. A rock struck the cobblestones just behind the puppy, to be followed an instant later by another.

Josiah leaned over and scooped up the puppy. "Whoa, little fellow," he said in a crooning voice. "Where are you going so fast?"

Just then a gang of young peasant boys dashed around the corner of the building with hands raised to hurl more rocks. They skidded to an abrupt halt when they saw Josiah. The young prince took in the situation at a glance. "Are you lads tormenting this poor puppy?" he asked sternly, taking a step toward the boys. The puppy trembled in his arms.

As one, the boys moved backwards. "She's just a worthless stray, my lord," one young lad answered defensively. "We were just having a bit of sport with her."

"Throwing stones at a helpless puppy is your idea of sport?" Josiah retorted angrily. "You ought to be ashamed! Off with you now before I take a notion to thrash the lot of you." The boys scattered like ashes in a stiff wind.

"You'll be all right now," Josiah reassured the puppy. Holding the trembling animal to his chest, he stroked it gently as he strolled down the narrow street.

"Aye, that's a fine puppy, my lord," a voice called to Josiah as the young prince passed an apothecary shop. Josiah looked over to see a tall merchant unlocking the door of the shop. He hurried over.

"Would you like to have her?" Josiah asked the man. "I just rescued her from a band of boys who were tormenting her."

The merchant looked the puppy over and then smiled

broadly. "Certainly, my lord. My children would love a puppy such as this." He took the animal from Josiah's arms. "You must be a lover of animals, my lord, to care this much about one small, insignificant dog."

Josiah shrugged. "I am, though I have never had a pet of my own." He paused. "Well, I did have a pet briefly, but I'm afraid it ended rather badly."

The man looked concerned. "What happened, my lord?"

"I had a peregrine falcon for a few weeks, sire, but it was killed suddenly."

"Killed, my lord? How?"

"A dragon destroyed it." Josiah said the words in a whisper.

"A dragon, my lord? Are you certain?"

"I saw it happen, sire. I was hunting the falcon when the dragon dived from the clouds and killed my falcon before my eyes." The young prince let out his breath in a long sigh. "Someday I shall kill this dragon, though it is a Cararian Greatwing."

The merchant looked at Josiah with a hint of misgiving in his eyes. "How will you find this dragon, my lord? That might prove quite a difficult task, you know." He stroked the puppy's ears.

Josiah shrugged. "The dragon will one day come to me. I—I hatched it from an egg."

The merchant raised his eyebrows. "You hatched a Cararian Greatwing?"

Josiah nodded without answering.

"Then why would you desire to destroy it, my lord? You said that you are a lover of animals, yet you have no pets. Think what a magnificent pet a Cararian Greatwing dragon would make!"

Josiah was shocked. "Possession of a dragon is a violation of royal law, sire. And the dragon *is* dangerous, for a Cararian

Greatwing is the fiercest of dragons. This beast has already attacked my castle on two occasions. I tried to do battle with it and it nearly killed me, though it is only half-grown."

The merchant held his hand out and the puppy began licking his fingers. "Your words tell me that you are afraid of this dragon, my lord. May I suggest that instead of attempting to destroy the creature, you must assert yourself as its master; then train it to do your bidding."

Josiah shook his head. "This is a Cararian Greatwing, sire."

"Cararian Greatwings train as readily as any other dragon, my lord." The man looked Josiah in the eye. "There is no need to destroy the dragon. Once you have it trained and under your control, it will become your servant."

The idea appealed to Josiah, but he frowned in bewilderment. "How would I train a dragon?"

The merchant smiled. "I can show you, my lord." He turned toward his shop. "Give me a moment or two to present this puppy to my children, and then I shall show you just how easily a Cararian Greatwing is trained."

Fifteen minutes later Josiah and the merchant stood on a hillside six or eight furlongs from the village. "Why did we come out here?" the young prince asked.

"The other villagers must not see the dragon," the merchant replied, without further explanation. "Call it to you, my lord."

"Call it?" Josiah repeated. "How does one call a dragon?"

"Simply clap your hands together six times. The dragon will respond."

The young prince scanned the skies above the hillside. "But the dragon is nowhere to be seen, sire. How will it hear if I simply clap?"

"Call it, my lord," the other insisted. "The dragon will come."

Feeling just a bit foolish, Josiah raised his hands and clapped six times. Almost immediately the thunder of mighty wings resounded across the hillside. He looked up in amazement. High above him, a Cararian Greatwing dragon swooped toward the earth in a swift dive toward the hillside. The young prince felt his heart constrict with fear. "Sire," he called, "this dragon is vicious! What if it—"

"Assert yourself as its master," the merchant replied calmly.

"How?" Josiah asked frantically.

"Simply stand up to it. Tell it that you are the master. Give it commands and expect it to obey."

The dragon came in hard and fast, plunging straight for the young prince in a reckless dive. Josiah's heart pounded with fear as he stood facing the diving Cararian Greatwing. When the beast was barely a hundred feet above the ground, Josiah abruptly held up one hand and called, "Stop! Stop where you are!"

To his amazement, the huge beast immediately flared its wings and came to an abrupt halt. The enormous wings beat the air in thunderous strokes as the dragon hovered above the hillside.

"I am your master," the young prince asserted. "You are in my power and will follow my every command."

"Yes, Master," the dragon said meekly. "What do you wish from me, Master?"

"Alight at once," Josiah ordered.

The great beast obediently dropped to the ground and folded its wings.

The young prince stared at the dragon. The creature was now gigantic, fully sixty feet long with enormous, powerful wings that measured nearly fifty feet across. The scaly green hide now bristled with thick scales, each of which was larger than Josiah's hand. The dragon's cavernous mouth held row after row of teeth nearly two feet long. Josiah realized that the dragon, a fierce Cararian Greatwing, was now nearly fully grown. Such a magnificent creature, and now it was under his control.

"Breathe fire," Josiah ordered, pointing to a stately elm some forty yards away. "Destroy that tree."

With a mighty roar, the beast obediently sent a blast of flame across the hillside to strike the elm. The tree burst into flames.

"You see, my lord," the merchant said grandly, "there is no need to destroy the dragon, though it is a Cararian Greatwing. You have the creature completely under your control; it is now your servant. As long as you continue to assert yourself as its master, it will do you no harm, nor will it bring harm to others. As I said, there is no reason to destroy it."

"I thank you, sir," Josiah replied with delight. "Of a truth, I had no desire to destroy the dragon, though Sir Wisdom had told me that I must. Now that the dragon is my servant, I have nothing to fear from it."

The young prince studied the enormous beast. "I shall name you," he decided. "I think I shall call you 'Thunder', for your wings sound like thunder when you fly."

"That is fine with me, Master," the dragon replied meekly, bowing its mighty head slightly to show submission. "From henceforth I shall be called 'Thunder'. The name pleases me, Master."

Thunder spread his mighty wings and gracefully took to the air while peals of thunder resounded across the countryside. Prince Josiah stood looking upward, watching the dragon as it climbed higher and higher, finally leveling off several hundred feet above the treetops. It began to glide in circles on motionless wings, and Josiah noticed that the thunderous sound stopped immediately. When gliding, the enormous dragon made no sound at all.

"It's a magnificent sight, isn't it, my lord?" the merchant said quietly. "There's nothing quite so majestic as a Cararian Greatwing in flight."

Josiah nodded. "It's incredible to think that he belongs to me."

"Finest pet in the entire kingdom of Terrestria, if I may say so," the other replied.

"I thank you for teaching me how to control him, sir."

"I'm grateful that I could be of service, my lord," the merchant said, bowing slightly. "Shall we head back to town? I simply must get back to work."

Hours later, Josiah sat basking in the warmth of a flickering campfire as he enjoyed a grilled steak. He had dropped the hart with one shot from his longbow. Fifteen yards away, at the edge of the clearing, Thunder noisily devoured the rest of the deer's carcass, snarling and gulping and drooling huge volumes of slimy fluid as he ate. Josiah could not watch.

"A mighty hunter you are, my lord," Thunder said, between gulps. "One would have thought the hart beyond the range of an arrow, yet you took it with one shot."

Josiah said nothing.

"So we are not to return to the castle tonight, my lord?"

The young prince looked up from his meal. "You are never to return there," he said sharply. "You are far too large to enter my solar, so there is no reason to visit the castle. Ever."

The dragon lowered his head slightly, as if acknowledging his master's order. "Aye, my lord."

"When I want you I will call for you."

"Aye, my lord."

"But never at the Castle of Faith, do you understand? The castle residents must never see you again."

Thunder seemed to nod. "But will you return to the castle tonight, Master?"

"I may never return to the Castle of Faith," Prince Josiah cried bitterly. "I have been banished from the great hall until further word from Sir Faithful. Why should I return when I am not wanted?"

"I would heartily agree, Master."

Josiah leaned back and looked upward toward the starry heavens, sighing as he thought of the many wondrous times he had experienced at the castle. A great, cold emptiness seemed to sweep over his soul as he pondered the fact that he had been banished from the great hall, that he could no longer enjoy fellowship with the other residents of the castle, that his presence was not wanted. "What point is there in returning to the Castle of Faith?" he whispered bitterly. "Sir Faithful has told me that I am not wanted..."

A twig snapped on the hillside below the clearing, interrupting his melancholy and snapping him back to the present. "Someone approaches our campfire." Thunder's voice was a whisper, barely audible.

"Be still," Josiah ordered. "This visitor must not be aware of your presence."

At that moment a familiar figure strode into the light of the campfire.

"Sir Wisdom!" Josiah was startled. He threw a quick glance in Thunder's direction, but the dragon was not to be seen. The only indication that he had ever been there was the bloody, half-eaten carcass of the hart.

The old nobleman stepped close to Josiah and gripped him

by the shoulders. "Josiah, my son, I must warn you again that you must destroy the dragon immediately. Delay will prove costly."

The young prince felt a flare of resentment at Sir Wisdom's words. "We have already discussed this," he said hotly. "Why must you tell me again?"

"You make no plans for the dragon's destruction," Sir Wisdom said quietly. He glanced at the carcass of the hart. "Even now you entertain thoughts of allowing the dragon to remain, though this beast threatens the safety of the castle."

"Thunder poses no threat to the Castle of Faith," Josiah said evenly.

"Thunder?" The old man tilted his head to one side as though perplexed and troubled. "You have chosen a name for this beast?"

"His name is Thunder. As I said, sire, he poses no threat to the castle, nor to its inhabitants."

Sir Wisdom smiled sadly. "What brought you to that conclusion, lad?"

"I am his master."

"His master?"

"Thunder is now in my power," Prince Josiah said proudly. "Though he is a mighty dragon, I now have him completely under my control."

The old man laughed out loud. Josiah's anger flared again. "Why do you laugh at me, sire?"

"You deceive yourself, lad," Sir Wisdom said sadly, shaking his head. "Cararian Greatwings cannot be controlled."

"I have Thunder in my control," Josiah insisted. "He now answers to my bidding, and therefore, he no longer poses a threat to the castle, to me, or to anyone else."

"So you make no plans to destroy this beast?"

The young prince said nothing.

"Josiah, Josiah."

Feeling uncomfortable under the steady gaze of the nobleman, Josiah picked up a stick and stepped close to the fire, stirring the ashes. Sparks leaped upward to swirl around his head like angry bees. A tense silence hung heavy in the air.

"The dragon must be destroyed," Sir Wisdom told Josiah. "If you think you have him under your control, you deceive yourself. This beast will destroy you if you do not destroy him first."

Josiah said nothing. He continued to stir the ashes.

Sir Wisdom stepped between him and the fire. "Give me your book."

Josiah looked up at him in bewilderment. "Sire?"

"Give me your book. I want you to see something."

The young prince complied, reaching within his doublet and drawing forth the book. He handed it to Sir Wisdom, who opened it, turned to a particular page, and handed it back.

"My prince, I want you to travel once again to the Castle of Knowledge. Enter the first volume in the New Wing of the castle with your book open to this page. The things that you see and experience will prepare you for the battle with this vile beast that you have chosen to call Thunder."

Josiah glanced at the page in his book. He sighed as he recognized the passage. "And suppose that I have no desire to battle my dragon, sire?" He tried to keep his voice from betraying him, but a note of sarcasm crept in.

The old man regarded him with sad eyes. "This beast is not under your control, my prince, though at present you may think that it is. You are deceiving yourself. If you do not destroy the dragon, it will destroy you, and it will hurt others in the process." He stepped closer. "Your King, Emmanuel, would have you destroy this beast. To fail to do so is disobedience." He moved away.

Josiah's heart cried out at these words. He turned toward Sir Wisdom but saw only the blackness of the night. The nobleman was gone.

Chapter Seventeen

Josiah sat in the shade of a massive oak on the hillside overlooking a quiet valley. In the distance he could see a sleepy little village. To the west, a slow river meandered on a lazy course past the town and then disappeared into the forest beyond. From his vantage, the young prince could see a frenzy of activity on the riverbanks. A number of townspeople were clustered at the water's edge, but from such a great distance, they appeared as tiny ants and their voices were muffled and indistinct. He idly wondered who they were and what had drawn so many of them to the river.

He glanced upward. High overhead, Thunder circled the valley on motionless, silent wings. Josiah was unconcerned. The dragon was at such an altitude that he appeared as hardly more than a dot in the sky. Certainly no one in the village could recognize the dot as a soaring dragon.

He sighed. It had been two weeks now since he had left the Castle of Faith, two long, lonely weeks in which one dreary day followed another. He was no longer in the service of King Emmanuel, and his life held no purpose. He had no dreams, no goals, and no plans for the future. Life was empty. He felt like an autumn leaf that had fallen from the tree and was beginning to decay.

The bleating of a goat drew his attention and he turned to see a dozen of the scraggly animals being herded toward the village by a peasant and a young boy. Josiah laughed in spite of himself. The boy was small, perhaps three or four years old, but he carried a big stick and was busily chasing stragglers and attempting to keep them on the path by whacking them with the stick. "There now, Ahab," he cried, striking a huge Billy goat on the neck with the stick, "you have strayed from the path and must be set right. Turn now, Ahab, turn! Back to the path where you belong."

The goat lowered his head and turned toward the boy as though considering charging the tiny lad who was tormenting him so, but after two or three more energetic whacks from the stick he wheeled about and allowed himself to be chased back onto the path. The boy, pleased with his success, continued to pummel the shaggy beast.

"Hold up there, Jeremiah," the father called, with a chuckle. "Go easy with the stick, lad. Ahab is now going where we want him to."

"I was trying to make sure that he doesn't change his mind again, Father," the boy replied, obediently lowering the stick.

"He's on the right path now, lad. If he strays again, then use the stick."

Josiah laughed.

Two claps of thunder resounded across the valley and Prince Josiah looked skyward. "No, Thunder, NO!"

The dragon was dropping from the skies in a steep dive. Wings folded and claws extended, he was plunging directly toward the goatherd and his son. Josiah leaped to his feet and dashed frantically down the hillside, leaping over rocks and bushes in his haste to reach the scene. "No, Thunder! Stop!"

Leveling off thirty feet above the pathway, the huge dragon

swung his mighty tail, striking the hapless goatherd across the shoulders and sending him tumbling like a rag doll. Peals of thunder resounded across the hillside as the dragon rose in the air, wheeled about, and then plunged toward the boy. Josiah raced to intervene. "No, Thunder, NO! I order you to stop!"

Thunder seized the terrified boy in his talons and rose from the earth with the thunder of his mighty wings resounding across the valley. Jeremiah screamed in terror.

Josiah darted around the goats, which were now milling about and bleating in terror. "Let him go, Thunder!" he shouted. "I command you to let him go!"

The dragon dropped the boy, who landed sprawling in a dense thicket. Peals of thunder again rocked the valley as huge wings beat the air. Josiah turned, and at that instant was struck from behind and knocked headlong in the grass. Thunder had struck him with his tail!

Reeling from the unexpected blow, Josiah shook his head to clear his senses. He leaped to his feet, drawing his sword as he did. The frightened goatherd appeared at his elbow. "Save my boy, my lord! You must save the lad!"

"I'll do my best," the young prince promised between gritted teeth. "This beast has become a menace, and now he will die."

The dragon circled the bleating herd of goats as the valley echoed with the thunder of his mighty wings. Jeremiah crawled from the bushes and ran crying to his father. Prince Josiah crouched, sword raised, as he anticipated the dragon's attack. "Leave this man and his son alone!" he cried to the circling dragon. "I command you—leave them alone!"

Thunder bared his teeth and roared his rage. A blast of fire erupted from his mouth like a bolt of intense lightning, striking the hillside just above Josiah and setting the brush afire.

Josiah shook his fist at the dragon. "How dare you! Alight at once—I command you."

The dragon roared again, and another blast of fire issued from his mouth, streaking directly toward Josiah. The young prince saw it coming and leaped to one side just as the blast struck the spot where he had been standing. Josiah raced across the heather and leaped behind a huge boulder, trembling with rage. His own dragon was now attacking him!

A cry of terror echoed across the hillside, followed by the thunder of mighty wings. The young prince rose from his hiding place and peered over the rock. His heart constricted with horror.

With the thunder of its enormous wings rocking the valley, the fierce Cararian Greatwing dragon flew over the distant village. In its talons it carried a struggling, screaming child, and Josiah knew immediately that it was Jeremiah, the energetic young son of the goatherd.

"Help me, my lord," the goatherd begged, clasping his hands and falling on his knees before the young prince. "We must get Jeremiah back!"

"I'm sorry, sir," Josiah gasped, choking back his own emotions, "but there's nothing we can do. I—I have no power over the dragon."

The young father collapsed in tears.

Josiah's chest was so tight that he could hardly breathe as he hurried down the hillside and strode quickly toward the distant village. In an instant he had realized the awful truth—Thunder was not under his control after all, and really, never had been. He had been deceiving himself into thinking that he could control a Cararian Greatwing. And now the dragon—his dragon—had hurt another human being, and a young child at that.

The young prince could hardly bear the thought.

Chapter Eighteen

Prince Josiah trembled as he approached the village. The scene that he had just witnessed was too horrifying to even think about. He had just seen a fierce Cararian Greatwing seize a young child and carry him off. Even now, young Jeremiah's screams echoed in the prince's ears, and the memory tormented him. Worst of all, Josiah knew that he was at fault; that he alone was responsible for the hatching of the dragon.

The panic that had seized Prince Josiah seemed to subside as he reached the perimeter of the village. He passed a sagging gate and entered a quiet lane, marveling at the atmosphere of peace and quiet that prevailed. Had no one in the village heard the sounds of the attack? Had no one noticed the thunder of the dragon's wings or heard his mighty roaring? Could it be that no one had heard Josiah's shouted commands or the young father's desperate pleas for help? He found it hard to believe, and yet, there were no villagers running to see what was happening.

He stepped around a pile of rotting garbage and took a deep breath to still his pounding heart. There. That was better. A feeling that could almost be described as relief swept over him. The attack was tragic, to be sure, but really, was it any of his concern? The goatherd and his son were simply in the wrong place at the wrong time. It was too bad that the boy had been the victim of a hungry dragon, but there was really nothing he could have done to prevent it. It was none of his concern.

Moments later he approached the river. He had passed through the little village without seeing a single soul, and he found that just a bit strange. It was nearly noon, and any ordinary village would be swarming with activity. Where were the usual merchants hawking their wares, the craftsmen and artisans busily working in their shops, the children playing noisily in the streets? The village was quiet—too quiet—and he felt uneasy as he noticed it. Something was wrong here, desperately wrong, though he couldn't yet decide just what it was. But it was none of his concern, and so he pushed the troubling thoughts from his mind.

The young prince spotted a throng of villagers congregating along the banks of the river and so he hurried in their direction. "Care to build a boat, my lord?" a voice called, and he turned in surprise. A young peasant boy stepped toward him.

"What did you ask me?" Josiah inquired pleasantly.

"Would you care to build a boat?"

"A boat?" Josiah was perplexed.

"Here." The boy thrust a piece of green reed into his hands. "We build boats from the reeds that grow along the riverbanks, and then we race them in the river. It's great sport."

"It sounds like great sport," the young prince said agreeably. "Would you show me how?"

"Certainly, my lord."

The prince and the peasant knelt side by side in the sand as the young villager showed Josiah how to construct a tiny toy boat from the section of reed. Within minutes, the boat was finished. "It looks good, my lord," the boy said, examining the little craft that Josiah had fashioned. "It ought to sail well."

"I can hardly wait," Josiah said brightly.

At that moment, an elderly peasant woman approached. Her faded gown was tattered and mended, and her face was concealed by a threadbare shawl. Upon her back she carried an enormous bundle of sticks. As she reached Josiah and his companion, she suddenly tripped and fell to the earth with the massive load on top of her. A thin, trembling hand reached out from beneath the pile of wood. "Help me, my lord?"

Josiah turned away. "This is none of my concern," he said softly, more to himself than to any other. "She is attempting to carry too large a load."

"Will you help me, my lord?" the peasant woman pleaded again.

Ignoring the woman, Prince Josiah flexed the little reed boat in his fingers and turned to the boy. "Let's see how my little boat will do against these others, shall we?"

"I'm ready when you are, my lord," the boy answered. "Let's enter the next race."

"Prince Josiah!"

The young prince turned, startled at the sound of his own name. To his astonishment, the old woman upon the ground pulled back her shawl to reveal the bearded face of an old man. Josiah stared. "Sir Faithful!"

The castle steward stood to his feet and the enormous bundle of sticks tumbled to one side. "Prince Josiah, my son, whatever are you doing here?"

"Why are you here, sire?"

"Sir Wisdom sent me to find you," Sir Faithful replied, "though I hardly expected to find you here, of all places."

"Why would you not expect to find me here?" Josiah questioned. "Where would you expect to find me?"

"Josiah, my prince, do you not recognize this village?"

The young prince shook his head. "I have never been here before. How would I recognize it?"

"Oh, but you have," the steward assured him. "You and I once visited here together."

"Here?" Josiah looked around, perplexed. "But I have never been here before, sire. Of that I am certain."

"Look again. Do you not remember this river? The little reed boats? Did you not recognize the village as you walked through it? Don't you remember warning the reeve, Sir Neglect, that the mountain was about to fall on the village?"

The young prince frowned. A dim recollection was playing at the edges of his memory but it was almost as if his mind refused to bring the memory into focus. "I—I'm not sure, sire."

"Prince Josiah, you once told me that you would never come back to this village. 'When we leave here, I never want to come here again!' you told me. 'Nay, this would never happen to me! Not in a thousand years!' Don't you remember saying that?"

The memory was getting stronger, coming into sharper focus.

"Josiah, my son, you are in the Village of Indifference. How did you come here, my prince?"

"The Village of Indifference?" A variety of emotions suddenly overwhelmed him. "But—but how..." His voice trailed off.

Sir Faithful placed a gentle hand upon his arm. "Come with me, Josiah," he pleaded. "The Village of Indifference is not a healthy place for any child of King Emmanuel. Let's leave here immediately. I'll help you."

Josiah sighed. "How did I get here, Sir Faithful?"

"Let's leave this wretched village immediately," the old steward urged quietly. "We can talk when we are safely away from this dreadful place."

Sir Faithful and Prince Josiah followed a narrow footpath over the crest of a ridge and started down into an emerald green valley. Patches of snow lay upon the ground, but the grass was green and lush. The path led through a shady glen and made its way along the edge of a small stream. At the upper end of the glen, a majestic waterfall thundered down upon the mossy boulders at its base, throwing a fine spray into the air. A shimmering, translucent rainbow hung in the air over a deep, clear pool that swarmed with fish.

"What a beautiful place," Josiah observed.

"Let's pause to rest," the steward suggested. "We've come at least forty furlongs from the Village of Indifference. We can bathe our feet and catch our breath."

Two minutes later, the two travelers sat side by side on a large boulder at the stream's edge with their bare feet immersed in the warm water. "This feels good, doesn't it?" Josiah remarked.

Sir Faithful nodded. "It's quite refreshing." He paused, studying Josiah's face. "Care to tell me about the dragon?"

The young prince hung his head. "I'd rather not talk about it, sire."

The steward moved a little closer. "I'm not here to condemn, my prince. I'm here to help."

Josiah sat quietly for several long minutes. Sir Faithful waited patiently.

"I—I didn't realize how much trouble one dragon could cause," the young prince said in a low voice. He fell silent.

"Disobedience to His Majesty always costs far more than we intended to pay," Sir Faithful replied quietly.

"I never intended to take the egg in the first place," Josiah insisted, raising his eyes and looking intently at his companion. "The egg was beautiful, the most incredible thing that I had ever seen, but when I learned that it was the egg of a Cararian Greatwing, and that possession of a dragon's egg was forbidden by King Emmanuel, I knew that it was not for me. And yet, somehow, I found myself wanting the egg more than I wanted to please Emmanuel. It was as if the egg had gotten inside my heart and was willing me to take it. Does that make sense?"

The old man nodded. "The human heart is deceitful, my prince, and often desires that which is forbidden."

"I really wasn't going to take it," Josiah protested again, as if attempting to defend himself to his own conscience. "I just went back for a second look, and...well..." He sat silent for several long minutes, staring at the waterfall.

Sir Faithful waited without speaking.

"Life just hasn't been the same these last few weeks since I left the Castle of Faith. I feel so empty, so...useless! And it's all on account of the dragon."

Josiah turned toward the old steward. "This thing is getting worse and worse, sire. First that wretched dragon killed my falcon. Then he attacked the castle, and attacked me, and... now—" His lips began to tremble. "Now the dragon has attacked a goatherd and stolen his child, sire. And it's all my fault!"

"Disobedience to His Majesty not only hurts us, but it often hurts those around us," Sir Faithful said.

"What am I to do, sire? I can't go on this way. And I simply can't allow Thunder to attack anyone else! The dragon must be destroyed."

The castle steward was silent for several moments. "Ask for His Majesty's forgiveness," he said at last, "and ask him to cleanse your heart of this disobedience. Then go to the Castle of Knowledge and visit the Library of Learning. Enter the first portrait in the New Wing."

He held out one hand to Josiah. "Allow me to see your book."

When Josiah handed him the book, Sir Faithful opened it to a particular passage. "Enter the portrait with your book open to this page. What you see and experience will help prepare your heart as you endeavor to face the dragon and destroy it once and for all."

Josiah stared at the book. "This is exactly what Sir Wisdom told me," he said in surprise. "He told me to enter the first portrait in the New Wing of the library of the Castle of Knowledge, and he told me to open my book to this same passage!"

The old man nodded. "The dragon must be destroyed, Josiah. It has drawn your heart away from King Emmanuel. It has become a menace to the inhabitants of Terrestria, and its very existence dishonors the name of your King."

"Sire, I'm ready to destroy it," Prince Josiah said in a subdued voice. "This beast must never again attack another one of King Emmanuel's subjects."

Sir Faithful shook his head. "You desire to destroy it, which is good, but your heart is not ready. You must prepare your heart by spending time in the Library of Learning at the Castle of Knowledge. Should you go against the dragon with your heart unprepared, you would fail, just as you did before."

The young prince sighed deeply. "Sire, a few months ago I fought the dragon Authades in order to recover the Crown of Kuros for His Majesty. My heart was yielded to my King, and I rejoiced to be in his service. How could I have done such a thing as hatching the dragon's egg? Why is my heart no longer yielded?"

It was Sir Faithful's turn to sigh. "The human heart is unpredictable, my prince. Once your heart is yielded to the will of His Majesty, you must be careful to guard it daily. You must guard it against attacks by Argamor and his cohorts, and you must guard it against Palaios, your old nature. You must never forget that we are in a battle against evil, and you must be on guard night and day."

The old man stood to his feet and began to put on his sabotons. "Travel immediately to the Castle of Knowledge, my prince, and spend much time in the Library of Learning that you might prepare your heart for the coming battle with this dragon that you call Thunder. A Cararian Greatwing is no feeble foe and the battle will not be easy. Prepare your heart well."

Josiah stood up. "Sire, will you not go with me?"

Sir Faithful shook his head. "I must attend to another matter first, Josiah. Go to the Castle of Knowledge without me and I will endeavor to meet you there. When you reach the castle, if I am not there yet, spend your time in the library studying your book and preparing your heart. Send petitions to His Majesty to seek his direction in your studies. If I have not arrived when you are ready to face the dragon, Student, the castle steward, will send word to me and I will come immediately to be of assistance as I may."

He stroked his beard with the fingers of both hands. "Your book will guide you to the castle. Follow it closely, lest you be sidetracked and lose your way."

He gripped Josiah's arm in a gesture of farewell. "My prince, go trusting in your King. He desires victory for you even more than you do, and he will enable you to destroy the dragon. May his great love guide you and keep you." With these words, he turned and walked away.

Prince Josiah watched him go and then withdrew his book from within his doublet. "I will send a petition to King Emmanuel asking his forgiveness for my willful disobedience," he said aloud, "and then I will read for awhile to prepare my heart for whatever lies ahead." He opened the book, withdrew the parchment, and quickly wrote a petition to Emmanuel.

"His Majesty, King Emmanuel:

My Lord, my heart is heavy as I confess that I have disobeyed you. I have hatched a dragon, though I knew that possession of a dragon's egg is a breach of royal law. I humbly ask your forgiveness and pardon, my Lord, and ask that you would enable me to destroy the dragon forever.

Your son, Josiah."

Josiah rolled the parchment tightly and released it. As the petition shot from his hand to disappear over the treetops, he felt a tremendous sense of relief. It was as though a heavy burden had been lifted from his shoulders. He glanced toward the little stream and recognition swept over him. "The stream of forgiveness!" he cried happily. He waded out into the stream until the warm waters closed over his shoulders, and then joyously stepped back upon the bank. He sat down upon a log, feeling clean and refreshed.

"Pardon the intrusion, my lord, but may I join you for a spell? These feet of mine are just about to give out."

Josiah looked up, startled, as a youth slightly older than he sauntered toward the stream. The young peasant was extremely thin. His tunic was nearly threadbare and his sandals were so worn that it appeared that they would fall apart at any moment. He wore a sad, doleful expression; his dark eyes revealed a haunted, fearful spirit.

"What a day," he exclaimed with a long sigh, as if he were nearly exhausted. "My poor feet are so tired they feel as if they are about to fall off." He dropped to a seat on a nearby stump. "Ah. It feels good to sit down."

The youth studied Prince Josiah for a moment or two. "And where might your journey be taking you, my lord?"

Josiah hesitated. "I'm traveling to the Castle of Knowledge," he replied.

"For what purpose?"

"I plan to spend a few days studying the book given me by King Emmanuel that I might prepare my heart—" Josiah stopped, not wishing to say more.

"Prepare your heart for what, my lord?"

For some unnamed reason, the young prince felt compelled to answer, though the peasant was a total stranger. "I must prepare my heart for an upcoming battle."

"A battle?" The peasant seemed curious. "What battle is this of which you speak?"

"I must battle a dragon." Josiah's voice was little more than a whisper.

"A dragon? That will indeed be a fierce battle. What kind of a dragon—do you know?"

"This dragon is a Cararian Greatwing."

"A Cararian—my lord, surely you do not intend to do battle against a Cararian Greatwing! Are you not aware of the fact that no one in the kingdom of Terrestria has ever battled a Cararian Greatwing and lived to tell about it? My lord, do not attempt this. You will be killed!"

Prince Josiah drew himself up to his full height. "I am aware of the dangers that I face. I will battle this dragon to the death, for I am responsible for it. I will go in the name of His Majesty, King Emmanuel, and I will claim victory in his name."

The youth eyed Josiah, studying him as if sizing him up as an opponent. "You may not realize just how fierce an adversary you face, my lord. How long have you been a knight?"

"Not only am I a knight; I am a prince, the son of King Emmanuel himself. And I have battled dragons before."

"Royalty, eh?" The youth said the word in such a way that Josiah could not tell if he was impressed or mocking. "Then why not simply send your knights to battle this dragon, my lord?"

"I must face this dragon myself," Josiah replied, "for I am the one who hatched it."

"You hatched a dragon?" A smile played at the corners of the young peasant's mouth. He seemed amused, almost pleased, by this bit of information. "You, a son of King Emmanuel, and yet you have hatched a dragon? Do you not know that royal law forbids the possession of a dragon's egg?"

"You need not remind me," Josiah replied bitterly. "I am familiar with royal law."

The peasant laughed. "You say that you are familiar with royal law, and yet you admit that you have hatched a dragon. That tells me, my lord, that you have deliberately disobeyed His Majesty and chosen to break royal law. I would hate to be in your place when King Emmanuel learns of your disobedience."

Josiah frowned, irritated at the words of the young stranger. "His Majesty knows of my disobedience. And he has already forgiven me."

"I would doubt that, my lord. He'll have your head taken off for what you have done."

"I am his son," the young prince retorted hotly. "And he *has* forgiven me!"

"At the very least, His Majesty will have you banished from the kingdom," the peasant insisted. "You admit that your disobedience was deliberate. Is that not treason? Do you really think that King Emmanuel will let you get away with that?"

Josiah drew his sword. "Leave me at once," he demanded hotly. "Your words do not have the ring of truth, yet they trouble me. I will not have you troubling me further with your words of discouragement."

"As you wish, my lord," the youth replied, stepping away from the young prince. "But you should be made aware of what you are up against. You have disobeyed royal law, and King Emmanuel will not take that lightly. You will be punished, my lord. I would expect that His Majesty will disinherit you and banish you from the kingdom. Good day, my lord."

As the peasant turned, Josiah stared at him in a moment of recognition. "Wait! Don't I know you?"

The peasant paused and then shook his head. "I think not, my lord."

Recognition sharpened, and Josiah's anger flared. "I crossed the Mountains of Difficulty with you on my way to the Castle of Patience. You caused me to fall into the Valley of Discouragement. Aye, I know you! Your name is Discouragement, though you lied to me and said that your name was Woebegone."

Josiah advanced toward Discouragement, holding his sword as though to kill the peasant. "Be gone, you wretched blackguard, lest I run you through! Your lies shall not ensnare my heart today."

"My lord, you are mistaken—" Discouragement started to say, but Josiah took another menacing step toward him. The peasant turned and darted away into the forest.

Prince Josiah sat down upon the creek bank. The words of Discouragement began to replay themselves within the chambers of his mind. *"Are you not aware of the fact that no one in the kingdom of Terrestria has ever battled a Cararian Greatwing and lived to tell about it?"*

"You will be punished, my lord. I would expect that His Majesty

will disinherit you and banish you from the kingdom."

"You have deliberately disobeyed His Majesty and chosen to break royal law. I would hate to be in your place when King Emmanuel learns of your disobedience."

"Do you not know that royal law forbids the possession of a dragon's egg?"

"I would hate to be in your place when King Emmanuel learns of your disobedience."

"Are you not aware of the fact that no one in the kingdom of Terrestria has ever battled a Cararian Greatwing and lived to tell about it?"

"You will be punished, my lord. I would expect that His Majesty will disinherit you and banish you from the kingdom."

"I am Prince Josiah, son of His Majesty, King Emmanuel, forever!" the young prince shouted, as if to drive the disheartening words from his mind. "I have been forgiven for my disobedience! I will fight this dragon in Emmanuel's name and in his power, and though it be a Cararian Greatwing, I shall be victorious!" But even as he said the words, doubts began to creep again into his heart. What if Emmanuel did disinherit him because of his infidelity? What if he went against the dragon and lost?

At that moment, an enormous hand reached down through the trees, gripping his body in a bone-crushing grasp and snatching him up from the earth. His breath was taken away as he was lifted to a dizzying height so rapidly that it felt as if he were falling upward. Terror seized him as he realized that he had just been captured by the Giant of Fear.

Chapter Nineteen

Prince Josiah's stomach tightened as the Giant of Fear snatched him high into the air. His whole body began to tremble and the blood pounded in his head. His chest felt so tight that he could scarcely breathe.

Clutching Josiah in one massive hand, the giant moved Josiah to within a few feet of his face. "One of the little people!" he roared. "Insect, what are you doing here?"

The giant's face was a frightening sight. Red hair framed a head that was almost as tall as Josiah's entire body. The nose was as big as a boulder. Below the nose was a thick red moustache as wide as Josiah's outstretched arms, and a curly red beard encircled a cavernous mouth. The eyes burned with rage like two oil lamps and Josiah found them terrifying.

Turning abruptly on his heel, the Giant of Fear moved swiftly through the woods with enormous, jolting strides. He swung his hands at his sides as he walked, and the young prince found himself swinging back and forth through the air in long, terrifying arcs.

In no time at all, the giant and his captive approached an enormous castle. Josiah recognized the structure immediately. The Castle of Unbelief! Pushing open the castle gate which stood nearly sixty feet tall, the giant crossed the courtyard and entered the forbidding castle. "Welcome back," he roared, shaking with laughter. "You have been my honored guest before, have you not?"

Still rumbling with laughter, the giant carried his captive along a shadowy corridor and into the great hall. Josiah's heart sank. Once before he had been held captive in this great hall for more than a week, imprisoned within an enormous tea kettle. But this time the giant approached the massive fireplace, opened a huge, brass-bound trunk close to the hearth, and flung the young prince inside. Peals of laughter echoed and re-echoed throughout the castle as he slammed the lid closed, plunging the young prince into darkness. Josiah heard an ominous click as his captor locked the trunk.

As he slumped against one end of the chest, fear settled over the young prince like a cold mist, paralyzing and terrifying in its intensity. He struggled to breathe. *"You have deliberately disobeyed His Majesty and chosen to break royal law."* The words of Discouragement came back to haunt him, echoing within his mind with such force that Josiah actually looked about to see if the peasant was imprisoned in the darkness with him.

"Do you not know that royal law forbids the possession of a dragon's egg? I would hate to be in your place when King Emmanuel learns of your disobedience."

Josiah put his hands over his ears as if to shut out the voice. "I—I have b-been forgiven," he stammered aloud.

"You will be punished, my lord. I would expect that His Majesty will disinherit you and banish you from the kingdom."

"King Emmanuel has forgiven me," Prince Josiah protested. "I have confessed my fault to him and asked his help in destroying the dragon."

"Are you not aware of the fact that no one in the kingdom of

Terrestria has ever battled a Cararian Greatwing and lived to tell about it?" Josiah began to tremble. The thought of facing the fierce Cararian Greatwing dragon was frightening in and of itself, but the memory of Discouragement's words brought the young prince to the very brink of terror.

"Use the book," a voice said softly, quietly, and at first Josiah didn't hear. The fearful thoughts continued to play within his mind, overwhelming and confusing him. He trembled in the darkness.

"Use the book," the voice repeated. "The victory is yours if you use the book."

My book! Josiah's heart leaped. *The Giant of Fear didn't take my book. I can escape the Castle of Unbelief, for I still have my book!*

The young prince withdrew the precious book from within his doublet and opened it. Immediately the pages began to glow with a pure white light, glowing brighter and brighter until the interior of the chest was ablaze with light. Josiah sat quietly as he read many of Emmanuel's promises found within the pages. A tranquil feeling of peace quietly stole over him and his heart ceased its frantic pounding.

After a few moments of reading he turned a page, revealing a golden key that glimmered in the light from the glowing pages, reflecting myriad points of light around the interior of the chest that imprisoned him. Slowly, reverently, he reached for the key. When he picked it up, he heard a sharp metallic snap. With the creak of rusty hinges, the lid over his head slowly began to rise until the chest was standing wide open.

Josiah stood to his feet. "Thank you, my Lord Emmanuel," he whispered softly. Leaping upward, he caught the edge of the chest and pulled himself up until he could see over the edge. Grunting with the effort, he managed to swing one boot up.

With a roar of rage the Giant of Fear entered the great hall.

"Insect!" he snarled, "How dare you open the chest? Get back in there, I tell you!"

Josiah scrambled to the edge of the chest and leaped to his feet. Swinging the book with all his might, he quickly transformed it into the sword. The giant reached down at that instant, but the young prince was ready. Leaping upward with all of his might, he drove the blade of the mighty weapon through the giant's heart. With a crash that shook the very foundations of the castle, the Giant of Fear fell to the floor.

Prince Josiah dashed for the castle door, which opened to him of its own accord. His heart was light as he dashed through the door and left the Castle of Unbelief behind. He glanced up just in time to see a magnificent white dove flitting through the trees overhead.

Josiah studied his surroundings. "I'm not sure where I am," he said aloud, "or which direction to take to get to the Castle of Knowledge."

"Use the book," a quiet voice said, and he looked up to see the dove perched in a tall aspen.

He held the sword against his side until it transformed into the book and then opened its pages. Holding the book aloft, he slowly turned it about until its pages began to glow. When he was facing due west the pages glowed with the brightest intensity and so he started in that direction.

After a walk of several hours Josiah paused as he crested a small hill. A quiet valley lay before him, bright with the warmth of the afternoon sun. To the right of the road lay an orchard of glistening crystal sculptures, apple trees sleeping peacefully through the winter with their trunks and branches sheathed in ice. To the left of the road, the afternoon sun glistened and sparkled on a meadow of wind-sculpted snow drifts. A crystal-clear brook laughed merrily as it crossed the roadway beneath a stone bridge and then meandered through the beautiful meadow. In the very center of the quiet valley stood a small castle of the purest white stone with a rainbow of seven colors shimmering above it, bold and brilliant against the deep blue of the cloudless sky.

Josiah took a deep breath. "The Castle of Knowledge," he said with a note of quiet satisfaction.

Hearing a noise in the brush behind him, he turned and found himself face to face with a band of dark knights. "You are not to go to the Castle of Knowledge," the leader of the dark knights challenged, drawing his sword as he stepped toward the young prince. Behind him, a dozen knights instantly drew their swords.

Josiah drew his own sword. "Stand back, emissaries of Argamor," he cried, "for you shall not keep me from my purpose. I shall visit the castle, for therein lies my strength and my victory."

"Then you shall die, foolish prince, for it is my duty to keep you from the castle." With these words, the leader of the knights leaped forward, swinging his sword in a sudden attack that was intended to end Josiah's life.

Prince Josiah was ready. His Shield of Faith met the steel of the dark knight, repelling the mighty blow. At the same instant, his sword flashed silver as it struck the knight, knocking him backwards. Quick as a flash, Josiah swung again, piercing his opponent's armor and inflicting a terrible wound.

The knight fell back, dropping to one knee and gasping for breath as he struggled to remain upright. "Fall on him!" he cried. "Destroy the knave at once!"

Josiah abruptly found himself surrounded by the entire band of dark knights, all bent on ending his life. "For the glory of King Emmanuel!" he cried, swinging his mighty sword with all of his strength.

In no time at all, the thirteen dark knights lay dead upon the snow. "Thank you, my Lord, Emmanuel," Josiah breathed as he sheathed his sword and started down the hill toward the castle. "Your strength has become my strength."

As he reached the castle drawbridge, he was met by Student, the steward of the castle, who shook his hand with his characteristic enthusiasm. "Welcome back, my prince," the young man cried eagerly. "It is good to have you at the Castle of Knowledge once again. You have come to study in the Library of Learning, have you not?"

"Indeed I have come for that very purpose," the young prince replied. "I would like to begin my studies immediately."

"And so you shall," Student agreed, leading the way through the main gate and into the castle itself. Josiah followed him through a doorway and then paused. He and the castle steward were standing on the polished marble floor of a room so immense that Josiah could not see the far end. There was no furniture in the vast room; but the walls were adorned with enormous, gilt-framed paintings that reached from floor to ceiling.

Though he had visited the library many times before, Josiah shook his head in renewed wonder. The library appeared to be twenty times larger than the entire Castle of Knowledge! How could such a huge library fit within such a tiny castle?

"You are welcome to visit the library as often as you wish," his host was saying, "and to stay as long as you wish. May your studies be profitable."

"Thank you, sire," Josiah responded, eager to enter one particular painting. "It is good to be back at the Castle of Knowledge."

As Student left him, Prince Josiah turned and strode swiftly across the vast chamber, scanning each of the enormous paintings as he passed. The scenes were familiar, for he had spent much time in the library in days past. Moments later, he stepped through a doorway covered by a thick veil and entered a second room nearly as large as the first. He paused before the first picture. His heart pounded with anticipation as he withdrew his book from within his doublet and opened it to a particular passage.

"Might I join you, my prince?"

Josiah turned at the sound of the familiar voice. "Sir Faithful! You were able to come, after all."

The old man smiled. "I hastened with my other business that I might accompany you in this study," he replied. "Shall we enter the first volume?"

The steward and the prince moved forward and stepped into the massive painting. A thrill of anticipation swept over Josiah just then, and he and Sir Faithful found themselves standing in the middle of a vast wilderness. Not a building of any sort was in sight. "Where are we?" Josiah wondered aloud. "We're all alone."

"Not quite," the old man said quietly. "Look."

In the distance, Josiah could see a lone figure seated on a small boulder atop a rock-strewn rise. "Who is that?" he questioned.

"You know him well," Sir Faithful replied. "Let's move closer."

As they approached the solitary figure, Josiah stared in astonishment. "It's King Emmanuel," he said happily. "What is His Majesty doing here?"

"His Majesty has been out here alone for forty days without food or drink. He is about to undergo a challenging test."

Josiah opened his mouth to ask another question, but at

that moment, the sound of a horse's hooves echoed across the wilderness. Josiah turned. Two or three furlongs in the distance, a lone horseman galloped at full speed across the moors. "Who is that?"

"Just watch," Sir Faithful instructed, laying a wizened hand upon Josiah's arm. "And remember, you are viewing an incident that took place many centuries ago. The approaching rider cannot see or hear you, so there is nothing to fear. Watch and learn."

The horseman reined to a stop some thirty paces from them, and the young prince cried out in astonishment. "Argamor! What is he doing here?"

"Just watch and learn."

"Emmanuel!" Argamor called, turning his enormous black warhorse about until he faced the seated figure. "You are hungry and weary, my lord, for you have gone many days without sustenance. It shows in your face, my lord."

Argamor dismounted and walked toward Emmanuel. "Why not turn these stones into bread and eat, my lord? You certainly have the power to do so."

King Emmanuel stood to his feet and Josiah saw that he held a glittering sword in his right hand. "Man shall not live by bread alone, Argamor," the King replied, "but by every word from their King." As he said these words, Emmanuel swung his sword in a mighty arc.

Argamor leaped clear of the menacing blade and dashed to his horse. He mounted hastily, as if in fear.

King Emmanuel sheathed his sword and walked toward the warhorse. To Josiah's astonishment, the King ran forward three paces and vaulted up to sit behind Argamor. With a snort of derision, the huge horse leaped forward.

Josiah turned to Sir Faithful with a puzzled frown. "Sire, where are they going?"

"Follow them," the old man replied simply. "Turn to the next page in your book."

Josiah complied and found that he and Sir Faithful were suddenly standing just outside the moat of a huge castle. "What castle is this?" he cried to his companion. "It is immense, and it is beautiful."

"This is a special castle in the city of Zion, a city that is close to Emmanuel's heart. The castle was built long ago for the glory and praise of Emmanuel."

Josiah heard Argamor's voice and looked up to see Argamor and King Emmanuel standing atop the battlements of the highest tower in the castle. "If you are the rightful Lord of Terrestria, cast yourself down, my lord, for your own book promises that you shall be caught safely in the hands of the bright ones. They shall keep you from even striking your foot against a stone." Argamor's voice rang clearly across the castle walls; Josiah could easily hear every word.

"It is also written in my book that the King is not to be tempted," Emmanuel replied in a powerful voice that rang with authority. Using his mighty sword, the King drove Argamor from the tower.

"Place your finger lower on the page, my prince," Sir Faithful instructed, "that we might observe the last episode in this drama."

Josiah did so and immediately found himself standing atop a high mountain. From the brow of a rocky cliff he could see vast regions of Terrestria stretching away in the distance. "All this is mine," a powerful voice rang out, and Josiah turned to see Argamor and King Emmanuel at the very brink of the cliff. "This entire kingdom is mine, but I will give it all to you if you will but kneel and pay homage to me."

"Remove yourself from this place, Argamor," King Emmanuel commanded, brandishing his mighty sword, "for it is written,

'You shall pay homage to none but King Emmanuel, and him alone shall you serve.' Now leave me." With the power of his sword, Emmanuel drove Argamor from his presence.

The King sank down upon a large rock and was immediately surrounded by bright beings in shimmering white robes. Bearing platters of food and vessels of water, they began to minister to their King.

Sir Faithful stepped close to Prince Josiah. "What have you observed, my prince?" he asked quietly. "Did you perceive the reason for His Majesty's victory over this vile foe?"

Josiah was thoughtful. "His Majesty was using the book to defeat Argamor," he said slowly. "Each time he quoted from the book, Argamor was unable to stand before him."

"You have learned the lesson for which you came," the steward replied, and Josiah could see that he was pleased. "In the coming battle against the fierce dragon, you must yield to your King, make good use of your sword, and depend fully upon Emmanuel for victory. A Cararian Greatwing is the fiercest of adversaries. Only as you use your sword and depend on your King for strength can you hope to defeat this beast."

Chapter Twenty

Prince Josiah took a deep breath and let it out slowly. "I am ready," he said quietly to Sir Faithful. "I have spent much time studying the book at the Castle of Knowledge, and I have sent petitions to King Emmanuel asking for victory. I am ready to destroy the dragon."

Raising his hands, he quickly clapped six times and then drew his sword.

Ominous claps of thunder resounded across the heavens, echoing and re-echoing over the snow-laden treetops. Josiah's heart constricted with fear. He was about to come face to face with the enormous Cararian Greatwing, the fiercest of all dragons, and he knew within his heart that the battle would be the deadliest conflict he had yet faced. And yet, there was no turning back. The vile beast must be destroyed, and he was the one who must do it.

The dragon dropped from the skies on folded wings, streaking toward the snowy hillside like a falcon stooping for a kill. Prince Josiah caught his breath. The dragon was now enormous, far larger than when Josiah had seen him last. Peals of thunder rocked the hillside as huge wings flared wide, bringing the mighty beast to a standstill just a hundred feet above the hillside. A blizzard of swirling snow filled the air with the downdraft from the mighty wings and the trees of the forest danced and swayed.

"Thunder!" Josiah called, doing his best to keep his voice from quavering, "I have come to destroy you. You have drawn my heart away from King Emmanuel; you have attacked the inhabitants of my castle, as well as other innocent people; and you have brought dishonor to the name of my King. In the name of His Majesty, I will now destroy you."

"Fool!" the dragon raged, snarling huge jets of flame which melted the snow into puddles of water. "No one has ever faced a Cararian Greatwing and lived to tell about it. No weapon has ever been devised that can prevail against me, for my scales can turn the sharpest arrows and blunt the strongest spears. I can destroy you in an instant. Foolish prince, do not arouse my anger, for I will destroy you with one blast from my nostrils."

"Today I shall destroy you once and for all," Josiah answered fearlessly, "for I bear the mighty sword of Emmanuel. Never again shall you harm anyone within the realm, nor shall you again dishonor the name of my King."

Thunder gave a mighty roar that caused Josiah to step backward involuntarily. The dragon opened his enormous mouth, sending a plume of fire streaking downward. The young prince leaped to one side and rolled in the snow to avoid the deadly blast.

"Stand up to him, Josiah!" Sir Faithful called. "Use your Shield of Faith and your mighty sword. The victory is already yours."

In an instant, the dragon dropped from his hover. Swooping toward the hillside, he seized the astonished young prince in his talons; the enormous wings beat the air with mighty claps of thunder as the dragon rose above the treetops. Within moments, Thunder and his captive were thousands of feet in the air.

Josiah was terrified. He had come to fight the dragon, but just as before, the dragon had him in its power. He looked down, and his heart constricted within him. From this altitude, the Village of Indifference appeared as a collection of tiny toy houses; the river was a thin silver ribbon winding its way across a tapestry of mottled white. If the dragon should drop him, death would come within moments.

At that moment, Thunder opened his talons and dropped Josiah.

Terror such as Josiah had never known suddenly overwhelmed him as he fell through the frigid skies. Tumbling over and over, he plummeted toward the earth, screaming with fear as the rushing wind streamed past, buffeting and battering him. "Help me, my Lord!" he cried in desperation.

At that moment, he became aware of a swelling crescendo of sound. It was the noise of distant thunder, growing louder and louder until it seemed that the heavens were filled with the sound. He opened his eyes. Through the terror and confusion he slowly became aware of hundreds of winged forms making their way across the heavens. His terror increased. More dragons were coming!

But as the winged creatures rapidly made their way toward him, he saw flashes of color and light radiating from their enormous wings and realized that these were not dragons at all. His heart leaped. Lepidopteras! The giant butterflies had been sent by Emmanuel in answer to his desperate cries for help.

At that instant Josiah gently touched down upon a firm surface and he grabbed at it desperately. To his astonishment he realized that one of the lepidopteras had managed to swoop beneath him, catching him in midair. He crawled forward on the enormous abdomen, surprised to realize that he still clutched his sword. Gripping the powerful muscles that attached the enormous wings to the creature's body, he straddled the thorax and hung on tightly. With powerful strokes of the enormous wings, the lepidoptera climbed higher.

Josiah glanced upward. The rest of the lepidopteras had surrounded the dragon and were pummeling it with their wings and bodies. As he watched, the beautiful creatures took turns darting forward, striking the dragon with their bodies and then buffeting him repeatedly with their wings before dropping away to allow others to take their places. With his sixty-foot wingspan, the dragon was far larger than any of the lepidopteras, but he was hopelessly outnumbered.

Thunder roared his rage. Thrashing the air with powerful wings, he wheeled and tried to escape his attackers, but it was no use. The butterflies numbered in the hundreds, and they had him surrounded.

With a mighty roar, the dragon belched fire, directing fiery blast after blast at the beautiful creatures that were tormenting him so. But to Josiah's amazement, the flaming assaults had no effect on the lepidopteras. They continued to buffet the dragon.

The lepidoptera on which Josiah was riding drew alongside the dragon, and the young prince suddenly realized that the entire band of lepidopteras had skillfully driven the beast right to him. With a ferocious roar of rage, Thunder wheeled and flew straight at the young prince, snorting twin jets of fire. Josiah's heart pounded.

Leaning forward, the young prince raised his sword.

At that instant, a fiery bolt of lightning shot from the cloudless heavens above, striking his sword, and then leaped from the blade of his sword to strike the furious dragon just behind his massive head.

The dragon seemed to explode. Pieces of flesh flew in all directions. The mighty wings suddenly shriveled and collapsed and the lifeless body plummeted toward the earth like a stone. The smell of burnt flesh filled the air. Josiah leaned over just in time to see the enormous carcass strike the hillside below, sending a spray of snow in all directions.

Josiah's winged mount abruptly folded his wings and spiraled downward to land on the hillside less than fifty yards from the dragon's remains. "Thank you, my Lord, Emmanuel," the young prince said softly as he stepped from the back of the lepidoptera. "Alone, I could never have prevailed against this vile beast."

He looked skyward as the band of lepidopteras winged their way across the heavens, flashing brilliant rainbows of color and light from their mighty wings. A lump arose in his throat. "Thank you, Your Majesty," he said quietly, "for I would have perished if you had not sent them."

Sir Faithful appeared at his elbow.

"Did you see what happened?" Josiah eagerly asked the old steward. "A bolt of lightning killed the dragon! There's not a cloud in the sky, yet a bolt of lightning came down out of nowhere and struck my sword, then glanced off and hit the dragon. Where do you suppose the lightning came from?"

Sir Faithful shook his head. "There is no supposing about it, my prince. His Majesty knew that you would never prevail against the dragon, though you were ready and willing. In his great love for you, Emmanuel chose to slay the dragon himself in order to spare you."

"King Emmanuel did that?" Josiah was astonished. "I didn't realize that he has that much power."

"Emmanuel's power is limitless," the old man replied. "What you saw today is merely the slightest token of his power."

Prince Josiah stepped over to the body of the dragon and a shudder of revulsion swept over him. As he watched in horrified fascination, the dragon's scales slowly turned a horrid shade of green. One by one they began to fall off, dropping to the snowy ground with sizzling sounds and then disintegrating. Within moments, the gigantic carcass was completely stripped of its scales. The body began to disintegrate, collapsing upon itself and melting away into a sticky puddle of slime. A puff of smoke appeared, and then a thick cloud of smoke billowed upward from the puddle. When the smoke cleared there was nothing left but a dark stain in the snow.

The young prince stepped closer. "Not much remains of the mighty dragon," he remarked, suddenly experiencing a refreshing sense of relief. "Though he was a Cararian Greatwing, Emmanuel gave me victory over him. Thunder shall trouble me no more."

Sir Faithful trudged through the snow to join him. "My prince, let's go home to the Castle of Faith," he said quietly. "This dragon is now but a memory."

Glossary

Bailey: the courtyard in a castle.
Barbican: the space or courtyard between the inner and outer walls of a castle.
Bate: in falconry, to hunt from a stand or from the hand of the falconer.
Battlement: on castle walls, a parapet with openings behind which archers would shelter when defending the castle.
Bind: to catch prey while in flight.
Castle: a fortified building or complex of buildings, used both for defense and as the residence for the lord of the surrounding land.
Coat of arms: an arrangement of heraldic emblems, usually depicted on a shield or standard, indicating ancestry and position.
Creance: a light cord attached to the leg of a falcon.
Crenel: one of the gaps or open spaces between the merlons of a battlement.
Curtain: the protective wall of a castle.
Doublet: a close-fitting garment worn by men.
Fletching: feathers at the rear end of an arrow that help provide accuracy in shooting.

Furlong: a measurement of distance equal to one-eighth of a mile.

Garrison: a group of soldiers stationed in a castle.

Gatehouse: a fortified structure built over the gateway to a castle.

Great hall: the room in a castle where the meals were served and the main events of the day occurred.

Jerkin: a close-fitting jacket or short coat.

Jess: a short strap fastened around the leg of a falcon.

Keep: the main tower or building of a castle.

Lance: a thrusting weapon with a long wooden shaft and a sharp metal point.

Longbow: a hand-drawn wooden bow 5½ to 6 feet tall.

Lute: a stringed musical instrument having a long, fretted neck and a hollow, pear-shaped body.

Lyre: a musical instrument consisting of a sound box with two curving arms carrying a cross bar from which strings are stretched to the sound box.

Merlon: the rising part of a crenallated wall or battlement.

Minstrel: a traveling entertainer who sang and recited poetry.

Portcullis: a heavy wooden grating covered with iron and suspended on chains above the gateway or any doorway of a castle. The portcullis could be lowered quickly to seal off an entrance if the castle was attacked.

Reeve: an appointed official responsible for the security and welfare of a town or region.

Saboton: pointed shoes made of steel to protect the feet of a knight in battle.

Salet: a protective helmet usually made of steel, worn by knights in combat.

Sentry walk: a platform or walkway around the inside top of a castle curtain used by guards, lookouts and archers defending a castle.

Solar: a private sitting room or bedroom designated for royalty or nobility.

Standard: a long, tapering flag or ensign, as of a king or a nation.

Stone: a British unit of weight equal to fourteen pounds.

Stoop: to swoop down in a rapid dive, as a falcon after prey.

Tunic: a loose-fitting, long-sleeved garment.

Trencher: a flat piece of bread on which meat or other food was served.

Castle Facts

- The word **castle** comes from a Latin word meaning fortress.
- Falconry, the use of falcons to hunt small game, was popular during medieval times. It was called "the sport of kings."
- Each social class was assigned a certain falcon or hawk to fly. Kings flew majestic gyrfalcons; serfs flew goshawks.
- A peregrine falcon dives at speeds close to 200 miles per hour.
- A castle was often a social center for nobility.
- There are five classes of nobility. From the highest to the lowest they are: Duke, Marquis, Earl, Viscount, and Baron.
- The wives of noblemen, and women who held titles in their own right, were classed, from highest to lowest, as: Duchess, Marchioness, Countess, Viscountess, and Baroness.
- A nobleman's title usually passed to his oldest son. If he had no son, it went to his closest male relative.
- Nobility could be created by royal orders called writs of summons.
- In most countries today, titles of nobility have been abolished.

Disobeying the King

Like Prince Josiah, every one of us has disobeyed and dishonored the King. The Bible calls disobedience sin, and sin always impacts us, just as it impacted Josiah. If you are a child of the King, sin breaks fellowship between you and your King and keeps you from being effective in the battle. If you are not a child of the King, your sins have never been forgiven, and your sins will separate you from the King for eternity. Here's how to become a child of the King and have your sins forgiven:

Admit that you are a sinner. The Bible tells us: "*For all have sinned, and come short of the glory of God.*" (Romans 3:23) Every person on this planet has done wrong things and sinned against God. Our sins will keep us from heaven and condemn us to hell. We need to be forgiven.

Believe that Jesus died for you. The Bible says: "*But God commendeth his love toward us, in that, while we were yet sinners, Christ died for us.*" (Romans 5:8) The King of kings, the Lord Jesus Christ, became a man and died for our sins on the cross, shedding his blood for us so that we can be forgiven. Three days later, he arose from the grave.

Call on Jesus to save you. The Bible says: "*For whosoever shall call upon the name of the Lord shall be saved.*" (Romans 10:13) Admit to God that you are a sinner. Believe that Jesus died for you on the cross and then came back to life in three days. Call on Jesus in faith and ask him to save you. He will! And when he saves you from your sins, he adopts you into his wonderful family. You become a child of the King!